STEALING IRIS

Sahara Roberts

From South Texas with Love,

Sahara Roberts

Copyright

Stealing Iris © 2020 by Sahara Roberts

Kindle Edition

In collaboration with M.R. Browning

Editing by Decadent Publishing LLC/Wizards in Publishing

Cover design by Sarah Kil Creative Studio / www.sarahkilcreativestudio.com

TABLE OF CONTENTS

CHAPTER ONE

DANTE

"We were fated to kill each other, Dante. The simple fact we're still breathing is already a win."

The first time Montoya said that to me, at the edge of an isolated field along the Rio Grande, it was like death herself was kissing the back of my neck. Having his voice filter in on the high-end speakers, filling the luxury BMW, brought the sensation back to haunt me. My business partner may be a dark bastard, but the things he sees in the darkness have made us a lot of money over the years.

"Open your eyes to the world around you," he continues, "or you will search endlessly and never find what you most desire."

"You know, I still don't get what you think I'm supposed to want."

Thanks to our consulting venture with elite criminal society, we have money, homes, private jets, and the freedom to do anything we want. For Montoya, that means staying at the lodge on my family's ranch. For me, a stay in Monte Carlo long enough to win and lose more than most people make in a year.

"You haven't enjoyed the company of a woman lately." Why and how he knows this is beyond me. We work the floor at our parties, getting to know our guests on a personal level. Sometimes it leads to more. Though, when

I take a woman up on an offer, we both know it's a one-shot deal, so there's no expectations or hurt feelings to get in the way. Everyone walks away happy, especially me. "I'd say you're ready to find your mate and win her love."

Over the years, I've learned to trust and even respect Montoya, but this thing about me needing a *mate* went over the line. Damn Mennonite. Even his voice, that old-fashioned, uptight manner, is getting on my nerves. "So now you're trying to hook me up?" I challenge, intending to derail his plan.

"Not a hookup, *amigo*." He tsks. "Something much deeper."

Which is why I always avoid the conversation. It's not the first time he's brought up the subject, and today I'm in no mood for this bullshit.

"There's no such thing as a perfect woman," I retort, without hiding my annoyance. My taste leans toward an experienced partner who's into sharing. While I've come across the occasional woman who can catch my attention, she hasn't been the complete package, the one I want to see again. It's always been the blink of an eye then they're all easily forgotten, and I like it that way.

"She exists, Dante," he insists. "When you find her, the world around you will come to a halt."

"I don't—" A sharp pain pricks just behind my right eyebrow, signaling the beginning of a migraine. "I...uh." The pinprick intensifies, throbbing until I have to press my fingers against the corner of my eye.

"What's wrong?" Montoya asks, sounding all too innocent.

"Headache," I shoot back. I keep the pressure against the curve of my eye socket as I maneuver through traffic. "Damn it." I need to get home and start working up files for the weekend.

"Hmmm. There must be a neighborhood market or convenience store where you can get something for the pain."

Up ahead, the sign for Gloria's Market lights up as the sun dips into the horizon. I hit the turn signal as I move into the center lane. "Gotta go, bro."

"Feel better, amigo." Yet I'm not relieved when I hang up the phone. Sometimes it's like that with Montoya. I feel like I'm missing something that's staring me in the face.

Turning into the empty parking lot, I pull my hand back so I can put the gearshift to park. The dull pain slices through my brain, which is actually an improvement. Damn Montoya. It's times like this when things get disturbing. Sometimes it's like he's picking through my thoughts and knows what's happening better than I do, even when he's a couple hundred miles away.

As soon as I step out of the SUV, I feel eyes on me. *Fuck.* Annoyed, I open the back and grab a dark cowboy hat I keep to shield my face when needed. The best part of living in this section of South Texas is having a guy in a cowboy hat, faded jeans, and expensive shoes stepping out of a vehicle priced at six figures doesn't seem out of the ordinary.

Pulling the brim low, I stuff the keys into my pocket and walk toward the entrance. A friendly faced caricature with a beer belly and beat-up straw hat beckons me inside, promising incredible savings. The place is empty, though the big-brother vibe doesn't go away. A quick glance from under the brim confirms cameras watching from above while oversized mirrors sit in the corners, offering a view from behind each aisle. A local Tejano station plays over the speakers, the singer encouraging the women on the dance floor to show off what their mama gave 'em.

"Hey there," a woman calls over her shoulder from the back of the store. "I'll be with you in a sec." She pushes a mop into a narrow hallway while several large fans send the smell of lavender cleanser throughout the building.

Signs hang from the ceiling, leading me to the far wall and a small but well-stocked medical section. Snatching up something for migraines, I head back to pay. The cashier, a young, dark-haired woman, darts around the end of an aisle, her arms held out to help keep her balance. Tiny feet shuffle across the wet floor in a pair of tennis shoes that might be as old as she is. If I wasn't so used to keeping my thoughts to myself, I'd grin.

She wipes her hands on the front of the boring, coffee-colored smock she's wearing as she tilts her hips to slide behind the counter. "Is that it?" she asks, running the box over the scanner before dropping it in a bag.

"Yup." I pull a bill from the stack in my wallet and hand it to her.

She stares at Ben Franklin then purses her lips. "Sorry, I can't take that." She points a slim finger to the handwritten sign announcing they don't accept fifty or hundred dollar bills.

"No problem." I drag out the card I use when I travel. It's one of those gift cards you load on your own so nobody can connect you to the purchase or location.

"Umm." Pushing back a curl, she flashes a smile that lights up her features for a fraction of a second before she shuts it down. "Do you need water or something else to take those?" she offers, her attention on a sliding-door refrigerator a few feet away. The same colorful graphic of an old man announces they have the coldest drinks in town.

I don't, but grabbing a drink will give me a few extra seconds to figure out what the hell is happening. This girl with the thick ponytail of curly dark hair is an innocent kid, mid-twenties or so. She'd run the other way if she knew I'm standing here wishing I had a better view of her body as she settles in behind the register. That didn't include what I'd do if I could reach out and touch. Any other time I probably wouldn't give a sweet girl a second thought. But today is different because Montoya put the idea in my head.

"Yeah, guess I do." Before I can step over, she backs up and grabs a tall Ozarka bottle. Fingers spread over the contoured plastic, she swipes it over the scanner, once, twice then again, only to have the reader fail each time. The tip of her tongue darts out as she pulls the bottle around to read the numbers off the bar code.

Mmmm, I know exactly how she'd look playing those fingers around my cock before bringing it to her full, pouty lips. Putting the card into the payment slot, I twist the lid open and take a drink. The icy water is a sharp contrast to the heated thoughts creeping into my mind.

With the image filling my head, I reach into the bag for the meds. After fumbling a bit, I tear open the box then drop the container into my hand, just as the music goes silent and the lights go out. Big, startled eyes meet mine in the dim light. The stray curls framing her face stop dancing around in the breeze as the fans power down. Her only movement is the quick rise of her breasts as she sucks in a breath.

My chest tightens, sending the echo of my heartbeat throughout my body. I study her eyes, thick lashes lowering as she looks anywhere but at me. The image of her beneath me, lips parted, curls laid out around her, gets the best of me. I have to shift so I can get some relief, because even my cock is heading off on its own. *Damn you, Montoya.* The place feels a lot smaller all of a sudden, as if we're in an elevator. Just the two of us… I've never been into the shy, quiet type, so I need to shut this down *pronto*.

Playing on her obvious discomfort, I check the front of the smock, my gaze lingering on the curve of a perfect breast as I look for a name tag and find nothing.

"So, no hundreds and no power for the card reader means no water and no headache meds. And I don't even know your name so I can plead my case."

She crosses her arms, glancing over, out of the corner of her eyes. "Yeah, well, life can be a disappointment sometimes."

Despite my best efforts, a smile tugs at the corner of my lips. Maybe there's more to the little innocent than I imagined.

Fuck.

*****

IRIS

We're facing each other, separated by the register belt, with my comment hanging between us. *Why can't I keep my mouth shut?* With no way to take back the smart-ass remark, I have to apologize, but I can't grasp a single word. Who wouldn't end up all stupid when you have a tall, hunky cowboy staring at you like he's starving and you're a Texas-sized T-bone. I nearly snort out loud. This guy is way too good-looking for description. His girlfriend probably has to chase off women everywhere they go.

"Sorry," I murmur.

His lips twitch. "I want a name, not an apology."

Heat wells up in my cheeks and travels down my neck. The promise of a smile doesn't help. My tummy does all kinds of flip-flops as green eyes with some wicked golden highlights stare back at me.

Compared to the slick, polished women he must date, I probably look like a troll doll, with my crazy curls doing their own thing. The one thing I hate most about being broke is not being able to buy my toiletries. I've done okay without makeup because I got my mom's looks, but I didn't inherit her long, straight hair. I need product to tame this beast, and I ran out months ago.

There's a lot I took for granted while growing up. I glance toward the panel by the doorway, where I'd drawn our mascot in colorful window markers. It's an image of my dad, only I gave him a beer belly and a shirt buttoned wrong. A small rebellion after I stopped believing in unconditional love. Now, it's like he's mocking me from above.

"It should be just a sec," I assure the cowboy, refusing to give him the answer he's looking for. Seconds tick by, and nothing happens. The silence is stretching out from prolonged to awkward. It feels like the building is completely empty, and I'd done enough restocking this afternoon to know it isn't. If I had the money, I'd tell him to go and pay for his stuff myself once the power's back.

One Mississippi, two Mississippi, three Mississippi... He's still looking. My toes curl, and I'm getting self-conscious enough I might do something stupid, like give him my name or talk uncontrollably. Thankfully, I can't think of a single thing to say.

A loud clatter comes from the back, and my shoulders slump in relief.

"Goddammit, Iris," Conny curses as he untangles himself from the mop bucket. I clamp down hard on my lower lip so I'll keep my mouth shut. Taking a deep breath, I exhale as the tension around us fizzles. I turn to the cowboy without feeling like we're the only two people in the world. "I—um, sorry about that." Did he hear me? He's staring intently toward the back, his shoulders tense, brow wrinkled in annoyance.

One more clunk, and a loud splash comes from the back. Ugh, now I have a mess to clean up. Hopefully, the water won't get inside the freezer. All I need is the smell of lavender Fabuloso coming out of the beer case.

Conny comes stomping down the aisle, the heels on his boots making enough noise to be heard in the parking lot. They're ostrich skin, with those little bumps that look like skin tags. With his skinny frame, you'd think he's a little kid wearing his daddy's shoes.

Conrado Villa, the son of my absent father's girlfriend. Olga seemed nice enough back when they first got together, though she spoils her kid like nobody's business. She kept calling him my "big brother," but the asshole has been my own little slice of hell since the first day she brought him around.

"What'd you do?" he demands, puffing his chest up to try and look tough. Of course I'm to blame. Who else could ruin whatever porn he'd been watching. The little perv should be manning the counter at the meat market instead of being on the laptop.

"Nothing," I reply in a tired voice. "The power went out."

He grimaces then glances at the customer. His neck snaps back so fast I could only hope he was slipping on the wet floor. Going a round with whiplash would keep him away from me for a while. His jaw goes slack, as if he's come face-to-face with his idol or something. "You Dante?" he asks, squinting as he searches the guy's face.

The cowboy keeps his expression neutral. "You got the wrong guy, man," he replies, shaking his head once. "Here. I've gotta get going." He drops the hundred on the scanner and backs up a couple of steps, all cool, then heads for the door.

I pick up the money, enough to feed me for weeks, reaching out to return it. "Hey, I can't take this—"

"Keep it," he tosses over his shoulder and keeps walking toward the exit.

My hand shakes as the bill practically burns my fingers. He's leaving ninety plus dollars behind to get away from Conny? It doesn't surprise me that someone like him wants nothing to do with Conny. It's nice we at least have one thing in common.

Dante stops on the floor mat, Conny at his heels. With the power out, the doors aren't going to move. His shoulders stiffen. "Damn it." His voice is low enough I barely make out the curse.

"You *are* Dante." Conny puts a hand on Dante's arm and turns to me, his excitement rising to where he forgets we don't like each other. "Iris," he says, without a lick of disdain. "Do you know who this is?"

The cowboy is looking at a spot somewhere above his head. For a second, I feel sorry for him. He'd already had a headache when he came in. I can only imagine how he feels now.

Conny's wide-eyed, oblivious as only he can be as to how much the man doesn't want to talk to him. He shakes Dante's arm, positively giddy.

I take a step back, my heart beating in my throat. If Conny's that interested in him, I'm better off somewhere else.

*****

DANTE

Of all the places in south Texas I could have walked into, I had to choose the one with a guy I've been avoiding. *There must be a neighborhood market or convenience store...* I'm gonna kill Montoya the next time I see him.

I did a workup on Conrado Villa several months ago. Despite Montoya's insistence he had something of immense value, I didn't find anything that could be of any significant benefit to anyone on our client list. He's a little fish trying to swim in a big ocean, way out of his league, the type who would need to save in order to pay for the membership to a club so exclusive we find you then decide if you warrant an invitation.

I searched his background, which includes friends of no significance, a broken home with little to no family. It did not include a job here, or anything to convince me he was worthy of consideration.

Yet now, here I am, trapped in a convenience store, with him clutching my arm as he tries not to pee himself. With limited choices, I do the only thing left to me. Exhaling, I glare down to where his hand covers my elbow then flick my gaze up to him. He has an oversized forehead taking up most of his head, the rest of his features scrunched at the bottom. He should have enough sense to not comb his hair straight back, but that's what he does, and he's added a meager soul patch to round out his look.

"Man, I can't believe you're here."

Holding his gaze is pointless. Those vacant eyes tell me he doesn't get it. Relaxing my shoulders, I pull my arm up to drink from the water bottle, taking my own sweet time. "You should have more sense than to announce who I am to the world."

His hand falls away, leaving me needing to scrub that spot clean. "Uh, sorry." He shuffles his feet. The heels of those gaudy boots scrape the floor, with the intensity of a knife on fine china. It just adds to my annoyance. "Missed it, man. But it's just Iris." He points his thumb over his shoulder. "She won't say nothing."

Iris. Her name rolls across my mind, gaining traction. The woman-child hasn't moved from the register. Gone is the cute, scattered look. She's not self-conscious or second-guessing herself, either. Instead, her eyes are open wide, a wariness about her as if she senses danger. She's waiting, a doe caught in the lethal gaze of a leopard.

Blinking, she leans away, breaking the spell. Apprehension is carved into her features. With a quick glance from Conrado to me, she clears her throat. "I'll go clean up the mess in the back." Pushing off from the counter, she's out from behind the register. A quick tug pulls the end of the smock down to cover her ass. The space between the smock and the back of her legs tells me there's more to see than meets the eye. The lovely Iris is hiding some killer curves.

She turns into the first aisle and, within a second, she's out of view. Her head and ponytail are barely visible above the top of the shelves. Checking the mirror is another disappointment. Her features are shadowed, masking her expression as she hurries to the back of the store. Pushing through the swinging door, she disappears into the darkness without a backward glance.

Conrado shifts, dragging my attention away from the intriguing Iris. While I've been watching her, every step of the way, he's been watching me. He knows. A shot of anger tightens the muscles along my shoulders. I almost forgot he's there. Even if it's for a second, in my world, that could be enough to end me. I haven't been so careless, in a long, long time.

Conrado heads to the register, and my heartbeat speeds up. My only weapon is a short blade. I reach toward my belt buckle as I watch his hands. He stops at the conveyor belt and snatches up the bill I dropped. "Here." He offers it up. "No charge."

Dammit all. I uncurl my fingers, letting my hand drop to a nonthreatening position at my side. If there's one thing I hate, it's being in somebody's debt. While I wouldn't mind giving the hundred to Iris, I couldn't leave him the money. He'd probably stash it away and give it back to me as part of the hundred-thousand-dollar membership fee.

Fuck. Fate's a bitch. "Look." I give a sharp exhale, resigned to losing time on someone I know won't make the cut. "Maybe we can discuss your interest in the group."

"Oh yeah!" His face lights up then so does everything around us, bringing the building alive. "Let's head back to the office." He turns on a heel. The door slides open and two customers come in, chatting about the inconvenience of the power outage.

"It'll have to be later," I warn him, eying a woman who dashes by. My gaze goes to the back, where Iris disappeared, but there's no sign of her.

"You know what?" Conrado follows my gaze. "I got a place we can meet up."

"Great." I think I managed to mask my disdain. He hasn't figured it out, but the guy's wasting my time.

"Hang on." He holds a hand up while he backs up to

the register again. Reaching across the machine, he tosses up the cover and drags out the receipt paper, pulling loose the roll to hit the floor and leave a growing ribbon across the tile. He tears off a piece and scribbles something before folding the scrap and rushing back over. "Here. Go by the office and they'll hook you up."

Taking the note, I shove it in my pocket and scoff to myself.

The little troll grins. "I'll make it worth it for you." Then he did the one thing that can change my mind: he looks over at the door where Iris disappeared.

CHAPTER TWO

IRIS

"Strip," Conrado says as he goes past me in the same room he always gets at the pay-by-the-hour motel.

My eyes widen as dread rips through me, twisting my stomach into knots.

"Why?" The question slips out before I can stop myself. In the time I've had to submit to his twisted appetites, Conny hasn't bothered with having me take my clothes off completely.

"Because I said so." He tosses the button-down shirt on the extra bed then pulls the wife beater over his head. The edge of his striped boxers are sticking up from his waistband, making him look like the gangsters on TV.

The gold chain around his neck clinks as the medallion slides down his chest to land on the name tattooed over his heart: Olga, his mother. He's always been a mama's boy, and she gives him everything he wants, including me. Though she made him stop screwing me...at home. Oh, it's not because she objected to what he made me do. Rather, she was afraid the neighbors might find out and think she raised a pervert.

Something's up. Conny's antsy, and it's putting me on edge. He turns on the old TV, set to a porn channel. He likes that, Asian porn in particular. Small-breasted women with narrow hips, tight butts, and straight hair get him off.

They're the total opposite of everything about me, yet I'm the one he drags to the room when he's in a mood.

For my part, I concentrate on the framed poster over the bedside table as he fucks me. Five different kinds of fruit. Three types of grapes, two peaches, two plums, three strawberries, ten raspberries. I keep meaning to check the library to see if two types of grapes can really grow on the same stem. It's the kind of thing going through my mind when I'm trying not to think about what I have to let him do to me.

"Come on, bitch. Get naked."

Moans filter in from next door while tacky porn music fills the room. My shoulders tighten until they ache. I let the messenger bag with my writing tablet and borrowed library book slide down onto the bed before I toe off my shoes. He goes to the dresser and pulls out a mirror and baggie from a pocket in his cargo pants. My heart sinks. He's going to get high. I can barely breathe as he keeps shaking the bag. If he takes too much, he may not be able to finish, and that's never good. Sometimes he blames me and smacks me around. Other times he's left me bleeding or unable to sit comfortably for a couple of days. He's a pig, but I have no real choice, not since he and his mother set me up.

"Let's get this party started." He sniffs, pulling the powder into his nostril then whoops as the drug hits his system.

I fumble with the first button on my top then go to the next one. My heart's in my throat as I drop the blouse on the bed and push the jeans and my high-cut panties down my legs. The whole time vivid images flash into my mind: the first time..., the pain, blood. His laughter when I said I was telling his mother and threatened to call the police. The sickening feeling when they showed me the film. The humiliation when I *had to* do it again.

Conny tosses his pants and boxers next to my clothes. He's hard. Hopefully that means a quick night. But then he wouldn't want me naked. I work the clip on my bra with a heavy heart.

"Come on, come on." He's jittery, shifting from one foot to the other as the drug pumps through his veins.

I pull the scrunchie off my ponytail, slipping it over my wrist. No need to give him something to hang on to. I drop my arm over my breasts. I can't help feeling exposed, but he doesn't bother to look at my body. Sometimes I've wondered what his deal is. Considering what he prefers, he might swing the other way. Which would mean he only does this to punish me for being my father's daughter. That hurts more than it should considering he's the reason I'm in this mess.

"Okay, let's see here." He jams two fingers between my legs, startling me into taking a step back. *No, no, no.* I fight the urge to bat his hand and run away. I spent too much time in my head instead of trying to relax and think about something, anything to help me get wet because Conny doesn't like to use lube.

"Shit." His hand curls into a fist, and I try not to flinch. "Okay, get on the bed." I place my knee on the mattress, shifting my weight while he gets a condom from his pocket. Ripping open the package, he rolls the latex on then gives himself a long stroke. The way he sucks in air sounds like a quick sizzle, and it's all I can do not to have my stomach roll. I hate that I have to do this, especially with him.

His head snaps back toward me, his eyes narrowing. I look away, coming back to the fruit, but it's not working for me this time. "Turn around." My back muscles stiffen, and I swallow hard. Desperate, my gaze darts around, looking for something that will open a space between me and the ugliness I have no choice but to endure. Light slants in from the window, dusting the green leaves in the painting with gold specks. *Dante.* My mind scrambled for every detail of that hot afternoon: his gaze, like a caress across my breasts, how he made my pulse skip ahead and my tummy flutter without even touching me. Something deep inside me wants to believe Dante is different, and I close my eyes, losing myself in that thought.

A loud clap fills the room a moment before the sting of Conny's palm spreads over my right cheek. My hand goes to the painful spot as I turn, my legs still folded. "Open up." He drops, squatting at the foot of the bed.

I pull back my hair, shoving a strand behind one ear as I spread my legs. *Dante. Dante. Dante.* Conny's fingers spread me wide and his head goes down between my thighs. His mouth covers me, and my body jerks. Not because this is so hot or because of the rasp of his wiry, meager facial hair against my skin. It's the instinct to get away, to fight this as I struggle to accept what's going to happen. *Why can't this be Dante, someone I actually want touching me?*

As much as I've read about how good oral is supposed to be, I don't get it. All I've ever known has been Conny's mouth sucking hard or the rough pull of his fingernails scratching long enough to leave me burning for days. My body eventually surrenders and releases the moisture he wants before it finally ends. Then he flips me over and—

The electronic lock on the door clicks, startling me.

Then the knob turns, and the door swings halfway open. My arm goes to my breasts, trying to cover myself as Dante comes straight out of my memory to fill the doorway. With my heart beating out of control, I watch as he checks the room, including the door to the bathroom before his attention settles on us…on me. Heat rushes across my face and down my body. Mortified, I push back, trying to scramble away.

Meanwhile, Conny sits back, unaffected. "Come on in, man." He signals to the bed next to us. "We're just getting started." His hand grips my ankle, giving me a hard stare, a warning about going against him, so I'm left with no choice but to move back. "Iris, you remember Dante." He spreads me open again, his nails digging into my flesh as his mouth comes down on me. I wince, unable to control my reactions with all the emotions running through me right now. The door shuts then, a few seconds later, the mattress on the other bed creaks, taking his weight.

Tears sting my eyes. It's one thing to have Conny do this to me, it's another for Dante to witness it. Yet I'm achingly aware of him close by, and my body reacts as I hoped. All I can do is let my head fall back so I don't have to face either of them. I shut my eyes for just a moment to escape into my little fantasy world so I don't freak out over Conny inviting someone to watch.

"That was quick." Blunt fingertips slip inside me, taking moisture to rub into my puckered hole. Clenching my teeth, I bring both hands behind me, bracing myself while he sucks at my clit one last time before pulling back. "Go on." He gives me a light smack so I'll turn as he comes up off the floor. Now, Dante is in my peripheral vision, his presence dominating the room. I can't help but glance over. Conny chooses that moment to rub himself against me. I look away, my neck and shoulders stiff. *Relax. Relax or it'll hurt so much more.* He spreads my cheeks, pushing into me. The first second is the hardest. Once things get easier, I can lose myself...except this time I have an audience. "It's been too fucking long since we did this."

It had been a while, and I fooled myself into thinking he'd gotten tired of me. Obviously, I was wrong.

Seconds tick by while Conny fucks me. He adjusts his angle, giving a single thrust.

"Hey, join in, man." My brain stumbles over his words. How can he do that? The blood's rushing to my head, making me dizzy.

"Iris needs to practice giving head while I go to town on her."

My heartbeat echoes in my ears, but Dante's deep voice breaks through. "Are you good with that, Iris?" Conny grinds into me, his fingers digging into my flesh, where Dante can't see. Tamping down my emotions, I assume the blank stare I'd mastered for those times when my thoughts risked earning me a beating, and nod. Dante leans forward, cupping my cheek while his thumb rubs my lower lip. He tilts my head up ever so slightly. "Let me hear you say it."

My gaze shoots to his, and I swallow hard again, knowing the wrong answer isn't an option. "Yes." The word is little more than a whisper. Dante hesitates, his brows drawing together. "Yes," I repeat, keeping my voice steady. The sound of his zipper fills my senses, and something between dread and anticipation takes over.

"Holy shit," Conny exclaims. "You're loaded, bro."

He settles in front of me, and I finally dare to look. Conny's right; he's big enough to suffocate any woman.

*****

DANTE

I wasn't sure what Conrado had planned, but I sure as hell didn't expect to find Iris with this idiot. Still, I'm damn glad I came. The ugly smock hid a lot. She has a body on her. Breasts that will more than fill my hands, a narrow waist, and an ass that'll make any guy forget his lunch.

This isn't my first rodeo, and, granted, I prefer to drive, but I'm not about to turn down an opportunity this tempting. Not when my cock jumped to attention at the doorway. Things only got more uncomfortable as I sat on the bed watching her. Sinful breasts pointed to the ceiling, her belly a smooth slide down to where shapely thighs cradled the guy eating her out.

Still, it bugs me that Iris keeps her face turned away. She did the same at the store, not facing me until she was caught off guard by the power outage. Her hesitation means she didn't expect anyone to show up. Is it me, a stranger, or is this her first time with two guys? Or both? That's why I asked, to make sure she's okay with taking my cock. She said yes, and despite seeing my size, she didn't backpedal.

Her hand surrounds me, stroking my length, like I imagined earlier. When she gets to the base again, her tongue darts out, tasting me, once, twice then swirls around the sensitive head. "I'm not very good at this," she says on a whisper.

I run my fingers through her curls, watching the curtain of hair sway, its silkiness brushing against my palm. "You're doing fine." I can wait him out. From the jerky moves, the guy doesn't have long to go then I can enjoy her. Truth be told, I'd like a lot more, but this is his game, and all he offered was a blow job, so I'll have to be good with that...for now.

My thighs and abs move with her play. Laying her soft cheek against my inner thigh as she figures out where to use her touch and her tongue. I want more.

Putting my hand to the curve where her neck meets her shoulder, I bring her in, having her take more of my cock. Her reflex kicks in, and she exhales in a rush, her thumb tightening against my balls.

The pleasure is short-lived because Conrado finishes with a sudden push, sending her sliding over my leg. "Watch it," I snap, the steel in my tone unmistakable. My focus is on her, despite the fact she could have done some real damage. "Iris?"

"I'm okay." Even having her hair in her face, the grimace is hard to miss. I help her regain her balance as soon as Conrado's off the bed. She settles in, her gaze following the soft caress of her hand. "Show me."

Show her? What I like? What I want? How inexperienced is she?

Her mouth comes down over me, and my questions fly out the window. She takes me in as far as she can while her velvety tongue runs the length of me. Her hand cups my balls while her hair dances over my thigh. The minute she adds pressure, my eyes are ready to roll back in my head.

I shift forward, needing to be closer to her mouth. She loses no time adjusting, her mouth going lower while taking me deeper.

She's a vision, doing everything she can to please me. Her spine dips, and I follow every move to where it meets her waist and her hips flare out to the shape of a heart. If she'd been at the edge of the bed the view in the mirror would have been perfect, showing me more than the underside of beautiful breasts.

I held back too long. My blood rushes, and my muscles tremble. "Iris…" I barely choke out her name before my orgasm rips through me with the power of an explosion. It's all the warning I can offer because she can't want a guy she just met coming in her mouth.

Though she's quick, she doesn't clear in time. She's singularly focused on me, using her hand to wring every last drop from my body. I run my thumb over her chin, wiping the spot clean. She tilts her head back, and the eyes that looked at me with such innocence earlier hold raw need and something deeper. Whatever it is she wants, I want to be the one to give it to her. Heat coils low in my gut. *Fuck.* Even though she just finished me, I push up, ready to stretch her out on the mattress.

Conrado comes around to pull on his clothes. "Damn, dude, rub that shit all over her tits." In that instant, the window into her soul slams shut. She pushes up on her side. "Hey," the asshole barks. "He's not done."

Iris stiffens, keeping her gaze focused on the sheet. "I

need to clean up." Her swollen lips make her pout that much more pronounced.

"Go ahead. We're done." Something isn't right here, but I can't put my finger on it. Despite that, I'm distracted by the sway of that perfect ass until she disappears into the bathroom, shutting the door behind her. The click of the lock echoes in my head.

"You sure?" Conrado holds up his hands. "I got the room for another hour."

Hmm, the things I could do with Iris in an hour. But they didn't include Conrado in the background. In seconds, I fit the pieces of a plan together in my head. "Yeah, let's go have a drink, and we can talk business." As expected, the guy's face lights up. It's what he's been hoping for, and if it gets him the hell out of here, I'm willing to give up the time. He moves around the room, struggling to contain his energy as I put my clothes in order. Reaching the dresser, he snatches up a small mirror and shoves it into his pocket.

Conrado picks up the keycard then hesitates, dropping it on the scarred wood. He puts two fingers to his lips and taps them on the TV screen before heading to the door. "Iris?" I ask, pointing to the bathroom, where the shower has just started.

"Agh, she'll make it home." He waves a hand dismissively. Pulling the door open, he checks to see if I'm following. I toss my keycard next to his and trail him out to the walkway. "Hey, man," he says, starting down the stairs in an excited rush. "I hear you got something coming up." He talks out loud, as if nobody else is around.

"Not here." I manage to cut him off before he says too much. While the nearest person is downstairs and a few doors over, the walls are thin, and the parking lot is filled to capacity.

"Yeah, yeah, yeah." His head is moving so fast you'd think he had a jolt of electricity running through him. "How 'bout Chili's? We can grab a bite, too."

"Yeah. The one on the loop."

"Yeah," he confirms, tripping over himself to get into his car, a sensible little Camry that doesn't quite fit his persona.

I keep going, pulling my phone as I reach the SUV. I stare at the screen, frowning, as if news of finding a lost hiker in California is the end of the world. "Something's come up." I feign anger, clenching my jaw for effect.

"Everything okay?" he asks, his hand hovering at the door handle.

"Yeah, but I need to cancel."

His eyes nearly bug out of his head.

"Postpone, not cancel," I correct. "Tomorrow." Unless things go really well. "Nah, Sunday. This might go on for a while."

"Not tomorrow?" he whines, as if someone took his favorite toy.

"Too many people around for the weekend."

"Ahhh, yeah." He taps his index finger at his temple. "I get it."

"Sunday at nine." We both get in our vehicles, and I

wait until he's ready to hit reverse before I pull out. I open the window while he does the same. "Bring Iris along."

He gives a thumbs-up and laughs. I drive ahead, not pulling into traffic until he backs out of his spot. I head north, seeing a chance to kill some time at the light, while he goes south. Within a minute, his car is lost in a sea of brake lights.

Perfect. Taking a quick left, I park at the strip mall next door. Minutes later, I'm walking out of the motel office with a new keycard and a box of condoms. While it's not an ideal location, I'm not up to waiting if she's willing to stick around. It's enough that I was able to maneuver the situation to my advantage.

I take the steps two at a time, shoving the card into the slot as my cock stirs, urging me to hurry the hell up. It's quiet on the other side of the door. Did she turn off the TV? Did she leave? Disappointment hovers around me, urging me to hurry. With one quick turn, I make it in the door at the perfect moment.

Iris is standing by the bed wearing nothing but a thin motel towel, her brown eyes open wide in surprise, a wild cascade of curls draping around her shoulders like a cape. She's the picture of innocence, an image I'd love to frame and hang in my bedroom. I'm fascinated. Something about her arouses my lust and a strange desire to know more about her.

"Turns out we're not done after all," I say, closing the door behind me.

CHAPTER THREE

IRIS

Dante. My pulse pounds as I stare at him. He's waiting to see what I do, and somehow I know he won't force the issue if I say no. For a few seconds, I consider that I'm able to refuse him. But honestly, it isn't Conny's anger that keeps me silent. I want this man. My body is responding to him of its own free will as a small flame of desire sparks deep inside me.

I try to process what I'm feeling, anticipation where there should be dread, desire replacing revulsion. For the first time I have a choice, the chance to experience sex on my terms. I get to explore his body, those strong arms I imagined around me earlier. My shoulders relax; my lips part softly as I drop my defenses. His answering smile is breathtaking.

He steps close and leans down, bringing me up on tiptoe with a hand at the back of my neck. My palm is high on his chest. The other climbs until my fingers are curving around the thick muscles of a full, rounded shoulder. His gaze roams my face. The minute his lips touch mine, my mind goes blank. I haven't kissed anyone in a long, long time. And even then, it was nothing like this.

We're close, his body making my insides vibrate from my chest down. We're moving back, until the back of my legs bump against the bed, but then he stops. "No, not here." He means this bed, the one we were on before with Conny. "There." He guides me while pulling his shirt over his head then tossing it aside.

His chest is a mass of hills and valleys, with a well-defined arrow of hair starting along the muscles that ripple across his stomach with every move. I follow the path with my fingers, dipping down past his belt to cover the area creating such a big bulge under his zipper. I'm touching him, yet the results have my body releasing moisture in a way I've never experienced.

The rough towel is tightening on my nipples with each breath I take. "Beautiful," he says in a husky voice. The way he's running a finger along my cleavage makes me want more. He kisses me again, pulling me close, like I'm the one thing he wants more than anything in the world. Then the corner of the towel comes loose. His body pressed against me holds it there, but Dante isn't willing to wait. The heat of his palm sears my skin, his hand going over and around my breast, holding the weight, like I'm his for the taking. He tugs the towel away from my body and drops it into a heap at my feet. As he explores my nipple with his thumb, I can feel the pull all the way down to my core.

"Get in bed."

I force my wobbly legs to climb in, stretching out under cool sheets. I'm not sure what to do next, so I roll onto my side, waiting for him. His eyes never leave mine as his jeans go down. *Can I take his length?* He's big. I know exactly how big. Part of me knows it'll hurt, but I want the memory of an experience I won't want to stuff into a dark hole in the back of my mind and slam a cover over it.

The mattress shifts as Dante gets in beside me, coming closer, claiming most of the bed with the sheer size of him. He's everywhere. His mouth, his hands, his chest, and even the leg he has between mine gives me an unexpected thrill.

I moan, low in my throat as his lips move along the side of my neck.

"You didn't come last time," he says, looking down between my legs where he's slipping two fingers. I'm wet, embarrassingly so, but I like how it feels when he touches me there. "Iris." His voice comes out slow and thick.

He lays me back, tasting the underside of my breasts. His heated mouth burns a trail across my stomach, licking under my belly button before moving lower. Setting a knee next to mine, he makes room between my legs. I tense as he settles at the bottom of the bed, positioning my calves over his shoulders. "You don't—"

His cheek, a smooth plane, slides along the inside of my thigh, the tip of his tongue tracing a path on my skin. The air between us is charged with a force stealing away all the oxygen.

Reaching the middle of the V he created, he runs his mouth over my swollen flesh, and I can't help but cry out. My breath rushes out with each sound. He tastes and licks, dropping kisses down my folds then pushes the tip of his tongue into my slit and rides up and over my clit. I come up, bracing on my elbows, but he doesn't stop.

Seeing him between my thighs, his arms wrapped around my legs, sends shock waves through me. He's relentless, centering on my most sensitive spot, the one making me squirm and has him holding onto me so tight. There's so much pressure inside me, and every stroke adds more. What he's doing to me is more than I can take and, within a few more passes of his talented tongue, I splinter. "Dante!" My legs tighten around him, my hips moving toward him then away with a loss of control I can't fathom. I swear he's torn me open, letting everything inside me escape in a vibrant rush.

My arms give out, dropping me back to the firm mattress. I need a bit to catch my breath. I'm boneless, every limb melting into the bed. *My first real orgasm.* God. I'm in a million little pieces that will never come together again.

Dante reaches for the box and rips open a foil package. He's huge, beautiful in the way only a man can be. The condom goes on, unrolling over and over until it covers the length of him. He stretches an arm, shifting his weight to move up my body. I push up on an elbow, turning away while preparing myself mentally to take his size.

"You like it from behind?" He palms the curve of my ass, moving across in what can only be called a caress.

"Conny does," I reply, focusing on the skin he's covering. I have my knee up, trying to concentrate on where to plant it when his hands wrap around me. He pulls my leg over to straddle him then brings me down hard, tearing through my cherry in a single thrust.

I cry out before I can cut it off, clutching at his back and shoulder as pain shoots through me like a sharp knife against my skin. After what I've gone through with Conny, I brace for a punch or a slap. Instead, Dante freezes.

Turning away, I bite my lip as realization washes through me. In one quick second, he's taken what's left of my innocence, and my only chance at getting my freedom back from Conrado.

*****

DANTE

She digs her nails into my shoulders and, in the back of my mind, I know she's drawing blood. I more than deserve the paltry wounds, after what I did to her. The rage that burned in me like a flash fire when she mentioned him fizzles out.

"Iris." Her name comes out in part question and part accusation. How could she not tell me? How was I supposed to guess, after what we were doing?

I hold her tight, afraid to move, afraid to shatter this moment and cause her more pain. I'm lodged deep, as deep as my hardened cock can go, and it's all I can do to keep my control. "It'll pass," I assure her. Not that I know how much it hurts, or how long the pain will last, but surely it'll pass because otherwise, women wouldn't have been fucking for generations.

She loses the stiffness in her spine and loosens her hold on my shoulders. I bring my hands up, rubbing her back, trying to offer comfort, though I'm completely out of my element. *Virgin.* She'd been a freaking virgin, and I took that away from her.

"Are you okay?"

"Yes," she answers in a tiny voice that makes me want to hold her tighter.

Her face is turned away from me, making my chest tighten. I lean back, trying to see if her expression matches her words. Another time I may pick up on cues and stressors, but right now I'm waging an internal war. It's all I can do to keep my body from following a natural reaction to a woman's tight grip on my cock. *Fuck.* I've never wanted something so badly and yet denied myself pleasure.

She moves, and I clamp her waist. "I don't want to hurt you..." *Again, more, anymore?* So, I let the words hang there. Whatever happens from here on is up to her because the one thing I'm sure of, is I'm not letting her go.

Her gaze meets mine, wariness swimming in the pool of unshed tears. She studies me, swallowing hard as her gaze roams my face. A tear spills, rolling down her cheek until I lean in and brush it away with my lips, taking the salty bit of her pain. We both freeze, and I'm surprised at what I've done. I never imagined myself doing something so intimate, despite what happened on the bed earlier. Right this minute, I'm completely out of my element.

Her inner muscles hug me, sending a shock through my entire body. "Aw, fuck, baby." Her eyes widen at my words, and she searches my face. Another subtle squeeze makes my fingers curl into her skin involuntarily. I narrow my eyes, but she remains the picture of innocence. We'll see about that.

I take her mouth, pulling her bottom lip between my teeth. Her hand comes up to cup my jaw, disarming me. I didn't bite, the way I planned to. Instead, I let her take the lead and join in one kiss after another. They're gentle, my mouth moving with hers, enjoying fullness until she opens to me. Now I can finally gain my footing.

My first taste of her lips is a new experience for me. Her innocent sensuality is hypnotic, as is the tentative eagerness of her kisses. Her nipples pucker against my chest, the dainty tightening buds begging for my hands to cover them, to help them along, providing the pleasure she seems to be seeking.

I cup the sides of her breasts, working my thumbs under each, curling my fingers over the top, and refusing to pull away. She shifts, gasping against my mouth, her back arching with the sensations she creates. I press my eyes shut to keep my balls from emptying. This woman kisses with her whole body.

I push up from a seated position, taking her with me to stretch out on the bed. Still kissing her, I press our bodies together, drawing out another gasp. I pull out, stopping with the protest coming from deep in her throat. Concern holds me still. "Did I—"

"Dante, please…" Her fingers dig into my back as her hips try to follow. Relief flows through me, along with a healthy dose of self-satisfaction.

"I'm right here," I murmur, sliding back into her welcoming embrace. As much as I enjoy this, I have to move, my body's demanding it. "Don't follow," I mutter. "Meet me halfway." She's quick to understand, enjoying the long, measured strokes, if her heavy-lidded eyes are to be believed.

My temple is against hers, my pulse echoing against her profile. I'm fighting my instincts to quicken my pace, to take her with the hard edge I enjoy. In the next second, she brings up her legs to hug me, nearly destroying me. My hold on myself slips, just for a second or two. No. Next time, next time we can fuck to the farthest extent of the word.

Her lips are parted. I can hear every breath she drags

in, every tiny noise in the back of her throat. I'm reveling in it, knowing I'm the only one to make her feel that. "Oh yeah," she says in a breathy voice then a quick sound of protest before she clutches at my back. Her legs tighten, barely giving me a warning before she arches against me. Her cry fills my head, flowing into my senses, but her pussy tightens, rippling along my cock, blasting me into a fierce, muscle-straining orgasm that nearly drags the life out of me.

Holy fuck. It's the only thing going through my head as I come down from one of the most intense experiences I've ever known.

Iris is wrapped around me, breathing as hard as I am. My face is buried in her hair and my arms feel like they're made of gel. It's the reason I haven't moved…at least that's what I'll tell myself. I should be cleaning up so I—we can get going, yet I don't want to move. Instead, I'm curious to find out if I kiss the spot by her belly button, will her skin smell like me.

Aw fuck. I'm so damn screwed.

*****

CONRADO

I'm in. Man, I can't fucking believe it took this long to happen. But he showed up at my place, so he must be impressed. I grin and blast the tunes on the shitty little stock radio on the car.

Iris is my ticket to the big time. That pussy is gonna open all the doors for me. I just have to wait for the right chance. Who knows, maybe Dante will want more once he gets a taste of her. He might even be interested in putting together a stable with me. High-class bitches, not some bunch of five-dollar hood rats.

I stop at the light, rolling business ideas through my mind. Dante and me, surrounded by hot bitches. Everyone stops what they're doing to look at us when we walk in. They want the chicks. You can see it in their faces as they watch us take over the room. They're imagining fucking them in every way possible. Something scratches at the back of my mind. Dante, at the store, checking out Iris. Then again when we were in the motel. He wanted to fuck her. I frown, thinking back. Dante's a player...but he didn't want more. He walked away without thinking twice. Doesn't make sense. Unless... What if he decided to go back for more? Iris wouldn't let him take her virginity, would she? Damn, she just might.

I can't afford to take the chance. I pull around the corner, tires screeching, and haul ass back the way I came. He wouldn't double-cross me, someone he wants to work with, would he? I speed up, blasting through a light just as it turns red then cutting around other drivers. Damn people think they have all the time in the world to fuck around.

The parking lot is still packed; one car can't even find a place to park. There's a red Mitsubishi sitting in the spot I left and a pickup in Dante's. There's a bunch of small cars, some pickups, a van, and even a lowrider. But I don't see the silver BMW he was driving or the dark SUV he was in earlier. I slouch back into the seat. Maybe I was wrong. But the light in the room on the second floor is on, and there's two shadows. I pull up to the end of the lot, past the office, and get out of the car, still staring at the window.

"Hey." Benny, the guy at the counter, sticks his head out the doorway. "The room's already rented."

"Gotcha." Doesn't surprise me. This place is popular on the weekends for a quick hookup. If you know how to play things right, you can get a discount for taking the room as soon as the previous customer leaves and using the other bed, as long as you pay cash. That way they don't need to clean up before renting again. I figure Benny pockets the money for all those deals. It's what I'd do.

"Sorry, man. Got an empty coming up in about fifteen minutes," he offers. "But it's full price."

"Nah." I brush him off with a wave. "It's all good."

Dropping into the car, I back up and head out to the street. Guess I worried for nothing. Dante canceled because he was headed out for an emergency. I gotta learn how to play it cool, like he does. He's a big man, with lots of stuff going on. The kind of boss I'm gonna be now that I'm in the game with him.

Gonna go back to figuring out what to do with the piles of money I'm gonna be making. Just gotta wait for Sunday night to work out the details with my new partner.

CHAPTER FOUR

IRIS

"I don't want to talk about it." Dante's wrapped around me, his arm coming down across my belly as the unasked question grows louder. He doesn't move, may not have even taken a breath over the last few seconds. Conny didn't tell him? Because he sounded shocked when he broke through.

Darker implications flash into my mind. If Conny offered me to Dante, he must be part of the big score in the planning stages. And I played right into his hands. Instead of offering some kind of protest, I go stupid and let him fuck me—even wanted it. Worse still, I enjoyed everything he did to me. Inside, the little girl who planned to marry in white squirms over what I just did. But then my father, who was supposed to walk me down the aisle, is nowhere to be found. My mother's dead after a long, punishing bout with cancer. The only thing I have now is a threat that will take away my freedom if I don't give in to whatever Conny wants. Tears spring to my eyes, tumbling onto the pillow before I can stop them. I blink rapidly, getting rid of the moisture. After the first time, I swore nobody would see me cry ever again.

What will losing my virginity mean to my future? What will Conny do now that I've been with a guy? Am I free? Is there more?

My stomach churns. He'd gone on and on about me being a virgin. Once, he called it his golden cherry and said

I would change his life forever. I just had to keep my legs together until he got ready for me to give it up; then I'd be of no use to him. At the time, I thought he meant I'd be free, but what did he say earlier? *Iris needs to practice giving head...* He can't think this will keep happening, can he? What if he plans to offer me to two guys at a time? I shudder, struggling to keep my tears in check.

Dante's lips touch the back of my head, startling me. His arm tightens, pressing me into the planes carved into his abs. "You're not okay."

No, I'm not. I'm wandering, alone, across the desolate space in my mind that offers no answers and no direction. Swallowing hard, I admit, "I'm not sure what to do." Which is as honest as I can be. I should be grateful my first time was with someone I find attractive. Someone I would have chosen to be my first.

Is Dante the one who can give Conny this new life? If so, who is he? What kind of power does he hold?

Dante rolls away, cool air taking the warmth of his skin from me. I shudder and hug myself. The loss of his touch shouldn't affect me so deeply, but it does. Squeezing my eyes shut, I push my feelings aside and focus on my reality. I can't let myself get comfortable with having a man around. Not that one has ever really been there for me. If my own father wasn't there when Mom and I needed him most, why would anyone else stick around?

"Iris?" Did he say something? My mind races. I've been so deep into my pity party I haven't been paying attention. Before I can figure out what to say, he's pulling me around to face him. My heart's beating hard enough for him to feel it. He leans down, dropping kisses along the side of my face until he reaches my lips. He's kissing me, taking his time, making parts of me wake up and take notice. Pulling back, he looks down at me with such tenderness, tears threaten again. "I would have—should have been, more careful with you," he says with conviction.

"Don't," I reply, shaking my head. "Just please, don't." Part of me doesn't want to know what the deal is with him and Conny. The other part of me knows right now I can't handle what it would mean.

He goes silent. The tenderness is gone now, if it was ever really there. "Let me go clean up, and I'll bring you a damp towel." Throwing back the covers, he gets out of bed without the least bit of hesitation or embarrassment. He's heading to the bathroom, his muscles rippling with every step, sending a wave of awareness through me. I had actual sex for the first time, with a man who looks like he stepped out of a fantasy. Even from behind he's impressive. That body's been next to mine, bringing me alive in ways I can't even describe in my head.

He's thought about me needing to clean up. Heat rushes across my face as I press my thighs together. "I-I can wait," I stutter, sitting up with the sheet held tight against my breasts. He goes on without slowing down. Oh jeez. The towel. Reaching down, I snatch up the bath towel I used earlier. The piece on top didn't hit the floor, so I can hold it against me without getting anything from this nasty carpet on me. The rough edge on the threadbare towel scrapes across the swell of my breasts. It's like a thousand tiny fingertips moving over my skin, tightening my nipples and sending an unexpected shock straight to my core.

My eyes widen, and my heartbeat quickens. What the heck is this? Does having sex flip some switch inside a person? Will I go from zero to horny every time I hold something to my chest?

The towel barely reaches my thighs, but I'm not as daring as he is when it comes to walking around without any clothes on. My inner muscles tighten involuntarily, making me relive the moment I moved while I was straddling him. I never imagined anything feeling like that, much less that a man would make that happen.

I know Conny's been killing something inside me, I just didn't realize how much damage he's heaped on me with his blackmail. Being with Dante, having him touch me with such tenderness, brought something out in me. It's like only he's been able to see the real me, the me I wasn't aware I've been hiding.

*****

DANTE

Iris is waiting, her bottom lip caught in her teeth and her attention somewhere far away. My conscience weighs on me as I curl my fingers into the warm, damp towel I brought. It's inadequate. A poor substitute for what I've become accustomed to. "Are you okay?"

Blinking, she snaps back to the present, pressing her arms a little tighter against her breasts. "Yes." Her focus stays at chest level while her cheeks turn pink. "I just need to get to the bathroom."

I hold out both towels, which she takes before sidestepping around me. The door shuts in my face, as if she's eager to get away. "You don't need to wait on me." Her voice filters through the door, and damn if she doesn't sound hopeful.

This is a little much, considering I couldn't know her...condition. I snatch my clothes off the floor and drag on my briefs and jeans. When's the last time anyone dismissed me like that? Never. At least I can't remember it happening. Yet this woman can't get rid of me fast enough.

To add insult to injury, I'm missing a damn sock. If I wasn't wearing boots, I'd leave without it. Reaching down to check under the bed, my gaze is caught by the faint pink blotch stretching out past the covers. Iris... The tension along the back of my neck ratchets up. Lost sock in hand, I plop down on the edge of the mattress, exhaling in a rush.

I stare at the bed. Part of me wants to bundle up the sheet so no one else will see it, but I don't want her to think I'm ashamed of what we did. I can't regret what happened because she's fucking incredible. Though I wouldn't choose a place like this, surrounded by dingy walls and cheap artwork, for her to remember her first time.

"Oh, you're still here." She's standing in the doorway, hand lingering on the doorknob. She must be used to Conrado taking off after a quick hookup. My first instinct is to trash talk him for disappearing, but I've done that, too, and it never bothered me...until now. It's disturbing to think there's even one area where we're similar. But I can change that, right here, right now.

"I'll walk you to your car then I'll be gone...it's not the best neighborhood."

The evasive turn of her head shows off the length of her neck now that she's pulled her hair up. Hell, I'm perfectly fine with her staying wrapped in a little towel. Sitting back, I cross my arms, taking in the view. She's beautiful, classic, real.

If she's going to get dressed, she has to walk over here because her clothes are right behind me. She realizes the situation within seconds, I know it from the slow exhale while her shoulders droop in resignation. Not exactly a great shot to my ego, but she's caving.

Padding over, she gives me a sideways glance. "You really don't have to wait on me."

"I'm walking you to your car." At this point, my stubbornness is getting the best of me.

"Then you'll be waiting a long time," she says, going by with a more self-assured swing to her hips. "Because I don't have a car."

I clamp down, grinding my molars. "So I'll drop you off." Yanking on my socks, I give her the opportunity to take care of the basics.

"Are you watching through the mirror?" The words slam down between us, a challenge I'll enjoy toying with.

"No," I assure her, shaking my head. "You're too far out to see you in the mirror," I tack on with a shrug.

"You're such a...man," she sputters.

"You say that like it's a bad thing." This time I turn. Her arms are stretched back to clip on a thin bra that outlines the crown of her nipples. The offering is temptation itself. A smile plays at my lips as I let my gaze trail down her body to the towel around her waist. The ends split to show her thigh at the widest part of her hips. Damn, she looks good, despite the disapproving twist at the corner of her mouth.

"They tend to be jerks." She yanks a scrap of purple fabric from the sheets and glares at me for a second before giving me her back. Stepping into the panties is enough to send the towel sliding.

Reaching out, I grab an edge and hold it up. She stiffens, checking behind her. I slip around and shake out the makeshift cover to give her some privacy. "Can't argue that." I didn't mean to be a jerk, but I've done things my way for too long to avoid the label. A nice guy would look away, but I can't seem to force myself to do so. "I'm a man. One who can appreciate the beauty of a woman's body."

That gets her to pause as she reaches out to pick up her T-shirt. Holding it tight, she lets her gaze drift across my chest.

"In this case, I know how yours feels against mine." I bring the towel down and gently hold her forearm, urging her closer until she's standing in front of me. "I know how soft your skin is," I say, wrapping my hands around her waist. My mouth is at her chin, nuzzling the underside, out to her neck, until she's pressed against me. "And I know how you taste when you come."

"Dante." The blush is immediate. I'm close enough to see the change in her coloring. But she doesn't move away. In fact, she puts her hands on my shoulders.

While I want to seduce her out of those purple panties, I can't be that much of an ass, knowing she may be hurting. "I need to know you're okay with what happened," I explain, pulling away to search her face.

"I'm fine." Taking a deep breath, she makes some sort of decision, and her body relaxes. "I never planned to die a virgin." She shrugs. "It just hadn't happened."

Until I pushed the issue. The words hang between us, unsaid. "All right." I slip down to cup her ass again. "If you're ready to go, we can get dressed." Neither one of us moves to put anything on, and my cock is onboard with whatever happens next.

"I, um, I open in the morning." So she has to be up early to go to work. But she isn't exactly rushing to leave, and I'm not about to hurry her along.

Strange, but I don't want her to go. I'll see her in a couple of days, yet I'm not ready to call it a night. "Come to dinner tomorrow night."

Her body tenses again. "I can't."

Irritation shoots through me. Though I don't need confirmation, I hear myself add, "Conrado." Why should it piss me off? Not like I didn't know shit's going on with them since I walked in on it.

"It's complicated," she explains in a tiny voice. Taking a step back, she flips the T-shirt and sticks one arm into the opening.

I should let her finish getting dressed, pull on my own shit, and leave. But I'm not one to let things go easily. I grasp the shirt, bringing it down like I have all the time in the world. It's all I can do to give her time to react and make a decision on what happens now.

Big brown eyes meet mine, searching my face, and ending when she gets to my mouth. The room is filled with the sound of her breathing, or maybe it's mine. If she looks up, she'll have the same heat in her eyes I saw earlier. Leaning in to wrap my arms around her, I kiss her lips, and her hands are on me again, holding on. In the next breath, I'm bringing her on the bed with me as I pop open the clasp on her bra and drag it down. Her bare breasts are on me before we hit the mattress.

Things are about to get even *more* complicated.

*****

DANTE

"Turn right at the corner," Iris instructs, stifling a yawn. After spending most of the night at the motel. I find myself in an unusual situation, driving through a quiet, middle-class neighborhood that, just a generation ago, was *the* place to buy. If her parents lived here then, they must have been well-off.

"The gray brick house coming up." We pull up to the curb, and she jumps out.

"I can wait while you go in and change," I offer.

She bends down, wetting her bottom lip while taking a quick glance over her shoulder. That evasive move tells me she's avoiding something, but I don't know what. "I can change at the store. Let me just grab some clothes off the line, and we can get going."

She rushes to the chain-link gate, opens the lock then goes through and scrambles up the drive. I pull the car forward to the edge of the empty driveway and watch her go past the extended carport. They have an actual laundry line. I smile, putting the car in park as I take in the rest of the place.

The house is older but well maintained, though the yard could use some attention. Will her father be out here later this morning, pushing a mower around to make the lawn look presentable? It's a sobering thought. Iris is a nice girl, living in a house belonging to a typical family. A place with parents and brothers and sisters. Not a place I belong, or that I'd willingly step into—ever.

I don't know what to expect from this moment, never having driven a girl home, much less bringing her by the next morning. Will the lights flip on any minute? Will her father come out with the proverbial shotgun, asking where I've had his little girl all night? Or is he expecting her to be with Conrado? Do they know the extent of their involvement? Will he guess I just took his daughter's virginity?

The house remains dark and silent, like the rest of the neighborhood. I blow out a breath. I've been in actual dangerous situations that haven't felt this tense.

She rushes back to the gate, taking a quick, if not nervous, check of the surroundings as she passes through. The morning breeze catches her curls, still damp from her shower. She transfers her clothes from her arm to her shoulder then locks up behind her. I reach across, pushing open the passenger door. When she ducks to get in, there's a slight smile on her lips.

"Thanks for waiting on me."

Totally worth it.

CHAPTER FIVE

DANTE

Sunday night took forever to get here. The restlessness won't go away, no matter what I try. It's dominated my time so I can't even get the second run done on the workups for this weekend's guests. And that's a necessity if we're going to meet their needs.

Iris and Conrado should be here soon. The last fifteen minutes could well have been an hour. Every car turning into the strip mall has me cursing Conrado for not being the one to arrive. *Damn it.* Why didn't I go by the store? If Tino wasn't driving me, I would have.

"You okay? You seem anxious," Tino asks without turning around.

"Yes. This guy's just taking his sweet time to get here." I should have checked the time because it's still seven minutes to nine. While Tino doesn't reply, he knows something's up. He's been with me too long not to be suspicious. Though he'll never guess I'm after a curly-haired prize.

Six minutes to go and there's still no sign of him. I run my hand through my hair at the temple. This is stupid. I can't believe I'm sitting here anxious for the sight of a woman I met just a couple of days ago. One I've only known for a handful of hours.

Five minutes.

Four. A Camry comes down the feeder road, the turn signal blinking his intention. I sit up.

"That him?" Tino asks.

"Yes." But a search as he drives by to get to the parking lot entrance shoots my blood pressure into oblivion.

"He's got someone with him." Nobody needs to tell me that. I can see the guy with my own two eyes. "Yeah. It's not who he was going to bring." Still, I sit here waiting, in case she's in the back seat. But as the two wannabes get out of the car, I know she's not here. Anger boils up inside me, pushing to be released like a geyser at its peak.

"What's the plan now?" Tino watches as the two morons draw near.

Damn Conrado. Only he could fuck up what should have been a quick discussion and a long dinner. One where I might be able to steal Iris away for the night. Now I'll need to take control of the situation, and I'm not in a generous mood. "Bring him here. Alone." Tino slips out from behind the wheel; his long strides get him to Conrado within seconds. I flip the overhead light off so I can watch his back then reach over and crack open the back door before sliding across the seat to the passenger side.

"Come with me." Even at a distance, I can feel the dangerous promise in Tino's voice.

Both guys hesitate. "Who're you?" The little weasel's voice holds a satisfying note of fear. If he knew half of what's in Tino's vast resumé, he'd be scared shitless. Tino backs up, opening the passenger door across from me as he goes by, but nothing happens.

"Now," Tino barks out. Footsteps. "Just him." Tino doesn't reach for a weapon, so things are going my way.

Muffled voices filter in from outside. "It's okay, man." Conrado's voice sounds shaky. His footsteps come closer, hesitating at the door.

"Decide what you're going to do," I snap, letting some of my annoyance slip through.

Conrado cranes his neck to look inside before he ducks back. After verifying it's me, he glances around the SUV to make sure I'm alone. "Hey," he says, relieved.

Tino gives him a thorough pat down.

"Rad?" The other guy's voice breaks on the question.

He looks over his shoulder, holding up a hand. "I'm good, man." His voice is back to normal. "Go inside and grab a table." Crouching, he slips in and sits back in the plush seat next to me. Tino closes the door then opens the driver's side. His dark shadow fills the front again, making Conrado hold himself away from the front seat, and Tino. Testing my patience, I wait, letting Tino start the engine while Conrado starts worrying.

"This isn't what we agreed to," I state, watching his companion hesitate at the entrance to Chili's. While I make sure my voice is modulated, Tino recognizes the tone. I turn in time to see his gaze flick to the rearview mirror, focusing on me. He knows I'm in the mood to be a bastard but doesn't know why.

"It's okay, man. Iz, he's my boy." As if his sad explanation matters. Tonight's dinner was for one reason, and he showed up without her. Two days ago, I had no qualms walking away. Now, that's not going to happen. Not until I figure out how Iris is tied to this motherfucker. Because the time I spent with her, more than I ever spent with another woman, isn't enough—nowhere near enough.

"You fucked up, again, *Con*-ra-do." My disdain at his name should have been enough to point out where he stands, but I've already witnessed more than one mental midget moment. "Anyone else would terminate business dealings."

"No," he says, wide-eyed. "You don't gotta do that."

"With anyone else…" I pause so he thinks we have some kind of bond he violated. "The options would range from walking away from the meeting to dropping you on the spot."

Conrado swallows hard, glancing to the front seat then outside before looking back to me. "I-I won't do that again." The reality's sinking in. Obviously, he's never considered the negative side of getting involved in the illegal trade. "Iris was tied up."

Of course she is. My stomach churns again.

"And Iz's gonna run with me," he rushes to explain. "Figured he should hear about what he's getting into." The smell of his sweat, a mixture of cheap cologne, desperation, and fear, reaches me in the enclosed space. While it doesn't fully satisfy, it's enough to make me feel better—at least for the moment.

"My part in this business is to set up the introductions for my clients. The people I deal with pay a lot of money for peace of mind. They expect someone they can count on. Someone who can maintain a certain level of discretion."

My tone makes it clear he isn't among the people I mentioned. "So, when I give you explicit instructions on when to show up and who to show up with, and you decide on your own to change the terms, you demonstrate to me I can't trust you. And if I can't trust you, I can't, in good conscience, let you be included in these dealings."

"Dude, no, don't do that," he whines.

Iris… The name crosses my mind, and I want her again. "The only thing I can offer is an anonymous connection." Tino shoots another glance into the mirror. All our deals are anonymous, not that he needs to know that.

"Okay." He nods enthusiastically. "What'd I gotta to do for that?"

"Put down a deposit." After some quick math in my head, I double the original total, a penalty for leaving Iris behind. "Fifty thousand dollars."

Conrado's face falls, and my satisfaction comes tumbling back. "We'll set the money aside for the client, in case things go wrong." We set aside a fund for every client from the membership cost and the nominal percentage we earn off each transaction. The paltry 50K wouldn't even cover transportation costs. "We're getting together this weekend. I might be able to consider you if you can meet the requirements." I can almost see the wheels in his head turning. "Can you do that?"

His eyes go unfocused as seconds tick by. "Maybe." Now I wish I'd tripled the amount. Damn it, nothing in his workup said he could pull together that kind of money in a couple of days. "If not, we can work something out, right? You guys set up auc—"

"I'm already giving you slack, Conrado," I point out, shaking my head.

"That's right, that's right." His leg bounces like a jackhammer. "Yeah, man, I can still get it together. Yeah, I think so," he assures me. "Can I call you?" The hope in his eyes is a tangible thing.

I should stop toying with this fool and put him out of his misery. Tino opens the door, and I take it as fate. "I'll check in on you later this week."

*****

DANTE

Tino glares at the rearview mirror so hard I look over my shoulder. Conrado is trotting up the sidewalk to meet *his boy* at the entrance to Chili's. The guy sags in relief at seeing Conrado back safe. The sad part is, we didn't even leave the parking lot yet. Clearly *Rad* and his buddy aren't a threat.

Tino's attention turns to my reflection once we hit the city street. The cold stare he reserves for his prey is all but measuring me for a headshot. "Do you plan on letting me in on what just happened?"

I owe the guy an explanation. From his point of view, it would sound like I just thoughtlessly plunged him back into the deadly world he walked away from. Since he's been with me, he's watched my back, either gun in hand or through a scope. I would never willingly put him in a situation where he'll need to kill someone if it isn't absolutely necessary.

Running my hand down my face, I exhale in frustration or maybe in defeat. "He just managed to piss me the hell off, man."

"So what's this about making some sort of an exception, with a deposit? And since when do you bring emotions into a business deal?"

My annoyance rises again. "I didn't think he'd be able to come up with the extra money." So either there's a gap in the information I have on him, or I'm missing part of the story. I'll reach out to Kassy, my IT guru, so she can dig through her sources and get updated intel on Conrado Villa. In our line of business, what you don't know can get you killed.

"So you won't be working with him?" Tino raises a brow.

"No. The guy doesn't have a chance in hell of coming near our group." We go to a lot of trouble to make sure the people we bring into the circle are a good fit. If there's any inkling of doubt on a prospective candidate, we move on. We can't risk having the law infiltrate the ranks. Well, the honest law.

"Wondered about that." His attention goes back to the road. "He doesn't seem like your usual crowd."

"No, not even close," I assure him. "The guy rubs me the wrong way." I shift in my seat, my mouth twisting in distaste. "I wanted to let him sweat for a while, but he got to me." I turn away, hoping my body language will deter him from asking anything else. But there's an expectation in the atmosphere, and I know what's coming before he opens his mouth.

"Is it something to do with Iris?" The words echo what's in my head.

And there it is. The topic I want to avoid discussing with anyone. Hell, even with myself. How can I explain she got under my skin after one night together? Maybe even after one brief conversation, while fully dressed. That just doesn't happen—not to me anyway.

"Montoya says Conrado would be an asset." *Don't ask if I purposely avoid talking about Iris.* Mostly because I might ask to drive across town to that house standing silently on a corner, in a middle-class neighborhood.

"Hrmph." The grunt is more along the lines of what I expect from Tino. "I'm having a hard time with this one. Something's off about him."

I had the same thought.

"Even that car he's driving doesn't seem right." True. The smart little four-door Toyota seems too sensible for him. "Then again, he could have borrowed his mama's car."

Okay, mama's boy would fit his profile perfectly. "I don't know what it is. He's playing things close, yet he can't keep his mouth shut and can't follow instructions."

"But Montoya says he's a go."

"That's why I haven't blown him off." It's a partial

truth, and might be enough to appease Tino's curiosity.

"Think you missed something in his background check?" He scans the area around us, making sure we don't have a tail before turning into my neighborhood.

"Yeah, I already tripped over a couple of things." I stretch back against the seat. "But we did the review on him several months back."

"A lot can change in several months." He shrugs. "Did you check to see if Montoya has anything new?"

"No." I hadn't given Conrado a thought, until I ended up stuck with him.

"We can see what he says tomorrow."

Something akin to embarrassment digs into me. The Monday before every party we drive out to the ranch and sit with Montoya, reviewing backgrounds. I document everything from favorite drinks to preferred cigars, and family ties to family feuds. Anything to put the client at ease and avoid possible confrontations due to unknowingly pairing up enemies. But over the past couple of days, I haven't gotten a damn thing done. "I'm rescheduling."

The suspicion in Tino's eyes claws at me from the rearview. "That's unexpected."

Heat burns at my collar. "I'm running behind with the files." Which is much better than explaining how I'd been sleeping off a sex hangover then been distracted by the oddest memories of a stray curl and the scent of her skin mingled with mine.

"I can hook up with Kassy later this week and dig into

Conrado's background. I'll send her the plate number off the car."

"Yeah, that sounds like a plan," I confirm, relieved at the shift in conversation. "A fresh pair of eyes may find something I missed."

"Or we'll find out something about his mama," he adds dryly.

I grin into the darkness as we pull in front of the wrought iron gate leading to my house. "Anything we can find on him will be useful." Especially if it includes anything to do with Iris.

CHAPTER SIX

IRIS

"Iris to the front, please. Iris to the front." Carol's voice, brimming with excitement and a little amusement, comes over the speakers. I frown. What is she up to? Tuesdays tend to be slow after a hectic weekend and Monday shoppers, so what does she need? Did I lose track of time?

I set a box of tomatoes on the rolling cart for restocking and wipe my hands on my smock. Sidestepping this morning's produce delivery, I head to the front.

As soon as I pass the heavy service doors, something flutters in my chest. Dante, looking shockingly handsome in a forest-green pullover, chats away with Carol. She's especially bubbly, which means she's flirting with him.

He looks directly at me as he finishes his conversation. "Excuse me," he says, without breaking eye contact then starts in my direction. My cheeks warm, and my insides do a few Beyoncé moves as snippets of the other night flash through my head.

Carol swivels around to check him out as he walks away, her gaze centering on the back of his jeans. Her hair slips off her shoulder as she leans across the counter to keep watching. The twinge, coming from somewhere deep inside me, slows my steps. We've grown close in the time she's been at the store, so I'm not shocked when she puts her fingertips to her mouth as she flicks the other hand.

Yeah, no denying Dante *is* hot, but I can't appreciate her teasing this time. Right now I want to smack her. I guess the fact Dante and I have been naked together changes some things.

"Hey." His casual greeting makes my pulse skip a beat. A killer smile plays peek-a-boo, popping up for just a few seconds before melting away. Long enough to let me blow off the rest of Carol's antics without plotting any serious payback.

"Hi." My voice gives out, only sharing the H in my greeting. I clear my throat, forcing myself not to wring my fingers or blush. "You looking for Conrado?"

He looks around at the fruits and vegetables section before turning toward dairy. "I don't look like I'm shopping?" he asks in his cool, laidback manner.

I raise a brow then take Carol's lead, checking him out under a thinly veiled pretense. "No basket, no cart, no list," I tick off on my fingers. "So no."

A ghost of a smile touches his lips. "Okay, maybe not. But I'd like a word with you, in private." His mouth on mine reminds me of how he looked when he kissed me. The idea of being in private with him warms me in ways I have no business feeling at work. "Can we borrow the office for a few minutes, or is he there?"

His suggestion lands on my chest like a ten-pound sack of potatoes. "N-no, he's out." I shake my head.

He frowns.

"But..." What? I've worked myself into a corner. He can't know I take pains to stay away from that area, and

Conny. I'm not about to explain my reason to Dante when he's looking to get me alone. However, he's handed me the perfect excuse. "There's a security camera in there," I murmur.

"Ah," he says, with understanding. So I'm right about why he wants privacy.

"Have lunch with me." It isn't exactly an invitation, if you go by the confidence in his tone. Yet in the background, Carol's giving a thumbs-up from where she's charging Mrs. Rocha, one of our long-time customers.

Heat shoots up my face. "Um…" How can I agree to go anywhere with him? Even if I had a dime to my name, I'm not dressed to go out. I put off laundry, so this morning I grabbed a faded-peach V-neck with dark leggings. Together with my old runners, my outfit probably doesn't cost what he spent on the shirt he's wearing. "Actually, Carol's scheduled for lunch in a bit," I explain, turning toward the register.

"I can wait…" Dante assures me, without looking at her.

"Go ahead," Carol says at the same time. "I'm good with going later."

"I can pick up something for her," Mrs. Rocha offers. The retiree, and devout churchgoer, spares a quick glance or two at Dante. If I'm not reading her wrong, she'll need to bring up how she was checking him out during her next confession.

It's hard not to grin. The image of getting thrown into a shopping cart, and wheeled outside, is both vivid and hilarious.

"We can bring you back something," Dante offers, the corner of his lips pulling up, "if you can wait." He finally looks over, now that he has her support in dragging me to lunch. "It's the least I can do for stealing Iris away early." Oh yeah, with that tone, he'll have her wrapped around a finger in no time.

"Sure." Carol waves at the aisle, a little jittery. "I work in a grocery store, so it's not like I'll starve." As expected, he charms her without really trying.

Dante waits, knowing he sidelined any reason for me to say no.

"You sure?" I ask sheepishly.

"Anywhere you want to go," he offers, his gaze flowing down me like a caress. Oh yeah, the guy knows he made the invitation sound as if he's offering something much more decadent.

Poor Dante. Letting me choose may get him more than he bargained for. We wouldn't end up somewhere you have to dress up. So, let's see how he'll do with a*nywhere I want to go*. "Okay, then." I untie the smock, knowing he'll have a look. "Let me wash up and we can take off." Even with my back turned, I know he's watching me walk away, and a little part of me is lapping it up.

*****

IRIS

Ten minutes after we're seated, Bunny figures out I'm at the café. "Ham and egg tacos, a la Mexicana," Bunny's voice bellows out the kitchen, right before she pokes her head out of the rectangular window, searching me out. "Ahhhhhhhh..." The loud and cheerful sound drags out, even when she makes it away from the line and out the swinging doors. The regulars, used to her boisterous personality, don't bat an eye.

"I-ris." Bunny comes barreling between tables, pulling off an apron printed with *If you stare more than a minute, I'll start charging* across her considerable chest. I have enough forethought to get up from the booth as she tosses the apron across her shoulder. Big, solid arms built from rolling out a mountain of flour tortillas every day come around me in a bear hug. "Glad to see you, *chula*." As always, she squeezes me to within an inch of my life. "It's been way too long."

The last time I set foot in *Bomberos* café, I dropped off Dad's missing person flyer. "Too long." I squeeze her right back. Being wrapped up in her arms is the first time I've felt normal in forever. A ball of emotion threatens to suffocate me, or maybe Bunny's just cutting off my oxygen.

"Let me look at you." She steps back, eying me head to foot with a critical eye. Her frown is immediate. "You've lost weight."

"Some." It comes from having an empty pantry at home, but I'm not about to share my situation. "The rest slid down to my hips."

"Nonsense." She gives my hip a quick smack. "Those

are breeder's hips, if I've ever seen them." She puts her arm around me and turns to Dante. "Am I right?" Heat travels across my cheeks, but I wouldn't shush her, as if anyone could. I love her for being herself. If I'd been prepared for Dad to date after Mom, I wish it had been someone like this woman who is all love and emotion.

"Bunny, this is Dante. Dante, Bonnie Bustos, or Bunny, as I've known her all my life."

He stands, reaching out a hand. "Ma'am."

"Oh," she says, looking him up and down before shaking his hand. "Good eye," she says leaning in, pretending to lower her voice. "You got yourself a nice one, hon." She winks in appreciation.

I'm sorry, I mouth to him, because not everyone's ready for such an immense personality, much less to have her focus her attention solely on you.

Dante leans in. "Don't let her fool you," he mock whispers. "I'm the one with the good eye." He actually winks at me, and my face flames. "But I'll have to get back to you on the hips." He answers so casually you'd think he hadn't been holding my bare hips just a few nights before.

Her laughter bounces off the far wall. "I like this guy."

Me, too. The words go through my head, but I manage to bite them back. Quick flashes of his hands on me, straddling him, having him pull me close, fill my head. While it was just a second of images, they result in an unexpected shot of heat between my legs.

The waitress brings our order, saving me from having to respond. "Well, I'll leave you to eat." She takes my hand, her expression gaining sympathy, so I know what's coming. "Any word on your daddy, *mija*?"

Tears threaten as the spotlight moves to shine on me. "No." I shake my head. "I'm afraid not."

She drags in a breath. "I'm sorry, baby girl." I swallow hard, avoiding looking in Dante's direction. "You're still on the wall over there." Out of the corner of my eye, I see him turn. Of course he would look over. Who wouldn't? Even I feel like a huge beacon is beaming from the picture frame and flyer up on the wall. "Though I didn't include the *puta* he was running around with." I couldn't help but smile. If Bunny loves you, you know it. Same if she doesn't. Clearly Olga didn't make the short list.

"Bo-*nnie*." The bellow from the kitchen carries across the crowded restaurant. Bunny rolls her eyes, giving me one last shake. "Lord, I really need to hire someone who can do more than one thing at a time," she mutters. "Got to go, baby. People to feed. Employees to strangle." She hugs me and winks at Dante before she makes her way back into the kitchen, pulling the apron over her head.

We both slip back into the booth, Dante still studying the wall behind the register. As much as I've been looking forward to this lunch, now that we're here, a knot forms in my throat, and nothing will get past it. Why would I think coming to a place I associate with my father would be easy? Yet, the question hangs between us, heavy enough to weigh me down. I'll have to explain because I know, at some point, he'll ask.

"My father...disappeared last summer." I pull my drink in front of me, running my thumb up and down the condensation along the side, steeling myself for the inevitable questions.

"He went across the river?"

"Yes." When he doesn't continue the conversation, I nearly sag in relief. It's one thing to know people disappear into Mexico on an alarmingly regular basis. It's another to have a loved one among the statistics. Worse when you wait innumerable hours for a ransom call that never comes. You could drive yourself crazy thinking about what he or she would have to endure. Yet people have the thoughtless habit of asking probing questions then ending in some horror story they heard about.

I force myself toward happier memories. "We came here all the time when I was growing up." The familiar surroundings set me at ease, welcoming me back like an old friend. "And yes, I usually order breakfast for lunch." He looks down at my plate with amusement.

"Bunny's from the neighborhood. Her mom lives across the street. She brought over food and checked on us when Mom was sick." When Olga started butting in, the visits stopped. "I was in high school when I finally worked up the courage to ask her to teach me how to cook."

"You cook like this?" he asks, his fork pointing to the *chile relleno* on his plate.

"To an extent," I admit. "I can't get the rice quite right." And it made me into a snob. "If I could, we'd probably have a lunch section at the store." Not that I'd be able to keep up with us down to a skeleton crew.

We both dig into our plates. He takes a bite out of the stuffed Poblano pepper, and his lips pull into a satisfied smile.

"This is good."

"I'm glad you like it." Bunny's place is always bustling. No matter what time we showed up, she always had customers.

"I notice your dad's name is Tony Gloria. So he owns the store."

It's sweet he said *is* instead of *was*. Though it's a little thing, most people don't catch onto how much it can hurt if you haven't given up hope.

CHAPTER SEVEN

DANTE

Iris slides toward the edge of the worn booth, pushing off in a little bounce that has her shirt catching under her. The soft cotton tugs against her breasts and waist to show off her curves by the time she's standing. I pick up the to-go plate while she turns, adjusting the shirt to drape across the curve of her ass, before heading to the exit ahead of me.

More than one man sits up straighter as she walks by, her hips swaying naturally with each step. I don't like it. A flash of possessiveness tears through me, and I drop a hand to her waist, letting them all know to fuck off.

For once, I can appreciate the ugly smock she wears at work because nobody else needs to be watching her beautiful ass. I reach above her to push open the door, and she glances back with the sweetest smile. Then I do something I haven't considered doing since puberty, I weave my fingers through hers, as we make it out of the little hole-in-the-wall café.

My dick's been at attention since Bunny got me thinking about breeder's hips. I had my hands around those bare hips…when I brought her down onto my stiff cock. Despite the way everything happened, I can't get the feel of her wrapped around me out of my head.

My focus should be on my surroundings, on any danger from the people we pass along the way to the corner parking lot instead of the damn pants she's wearing.

They've been in style for months, and women wear them everywhere, but few show off their bodies like she does, and I'm not sure she's even trying.

"Are you okay?" Those brown eyes look up at me with a shade of concern.

I study her face. Every angle, every slope of her features reveal her innocence. If she only knew where my mind went, to that moment at the motel when she was naked in my arms, her pussy filled for the first time. Is she the type to head back to the store on her own? Or will she use that knowledge against me, knowing how she affects me?

"I'm good." I pull out my keys and click the remote to turn on the truck from a block away. Hopefully, the air conditioner will kick in so everything can cool down while we drive back to the market.

We cross the street, hitting the pockmarked asphalt, to the far end of the parking lot, where I backed into the last slot. "Let me get the door."

She crosses her arms, her gaze covering my face as she tries to figure out what's going on. It only gets me harder. "You didn't like Bunny?" Her shoulders sag, and her voice lowers to a whisper, as if my opinion of her friend is important. Knowing what I think matters to her shouldn't affect me, yet it does.

I relax against the door, still holding the handle. "Bunny's great," I reply honestly. "I like how much she cares for you." Once I say it, I realize it's true. I like the relationship between the two women.

"But the tension around you is so thick I can feel it."

She got me there. "Is it me?" She hunches in a protective pose.

How the hell did I screw this up? I went from giving her space to making her feel like I'm pushing her away. I exhale in a rush, knowing I have to fix this any way necessary. "I guess maybe it is." She swallows hard, dropping her gaze until her lashes fan out on her cheeks.

How do you handle a woman who's both innocent and not at the same time? I haven't a clue. So the best thing to do is keep to the truth. "I want to kiss you." Bright, beautiful eyes stare back at me in an instant. "But you didn't seem okay with the idea." I shrug, laying my cards on the table. "I was measuring the consequences because I'm going to do it anyway."

She sucks in a breath, the vein at her neck fluttering with her pulse. I drop off the to-go bag on the seat then bring her in to take her mouth.

Kissing her is everything I remembered, the plump lips, the taste of the woman herself, and the underlying sizzle of something I can't quite describe. It's why I crave this, why I show up even though she shot me down when I asked her out. At least that's what I tell myself.

She draws away, just far enough to have space but still close enough for her lips to brush mine.

"I've been wanting to do that since I saw you," I admit.

"Mmmm," is all she shares.

I run the back of a finger down the side of her face, my cock getting harder at the fire in her eyes.

She doesn't move away. "Maybe since before then." I brush her mouth. "This morning." I kiss her again. "Or last night, while I was in bed."

Her lips part. "Is that right..."

"Then I show up to find you in this." I run my palm from the middle of her back to her side, then down to have the full curve of her ass fill my hand.

"My laundry's still on the line."

My mind fills with the image of a clothesline with little purple panties, lacy bras, and blouses that might barely cover the interesting bits. "Maybe I can steal you away for a little while." I nuzzle her cheek, working up her jaw.

"I can't," she says, the answer heavy with regret.

I push my hand in her hair, smoothing back the sleek curls as I tilt her head to drop kisses on the side of her neck. "You sure?"

"Yes." This time the word is tortured.

"I should have kept driving when I had the chance," I mutter beside her ear.

"And we wouldn't have eaten."

The setup is much too sweet for me to let it go. "Oh, trust me, I would have eaten." I run my tongue along her heated skin.

"Dante." Her answering shiver tells me she's reliving moments from our night together.

"You know as well as I do, if I reach between your

legs, I'll find your little clit covered in your essence."

She whimpers, and I run the pads of my fingers over the V of her legs. Her grip tightens on my arms then she leans into me from chest to thighs. The shock of holding her nearly knocks me on my ass. Every bit of this beautiful woman is within reach, and I'm trying my damnedest not to do something stupid. But there's one thing I can't control around her, and the tiny hitch in her breath says she figured out I'm hard.

"Are you sure you didn't wear this to torture me?"

"Promise," she says, her voice low and sweet. I run my hand over a plump cheek, bringing her close, to feel real pressure against my cock. Her whimper, deep in her throat, may actually be dissolving my brain.

I could easily bend her over the seat... No. Not like that. I could pick her up, drawing her legs around me as I bury myself inside her, and to hell with the rest of the world. Though I've never been one to give a damn before, this time jealousy itself stops me in my tracks. I won't share Iris, not with anyone. People around us might stop to watch and enjoy, or, worse yet, to judge.

I shift us into the corner, where the door blocks her from view. Her arms come around my shoulders, and I move up her body and under her top within two or three pounding heartbeats. Her bra isn't much of a barrier. I wrap my hand around her breast, fighting a mad urge to tighten my hold. I squeeze my eyes shut, but it only makes me much more aware of her nipple, a tight little diamond cutting into the center of my palm. *Get her back to the store...work...you're not doing this here.* Then she pushes into my hand, shredding the last of my good intentions.

"You're gonna be late."

*****

IRIS

He follows me into the back seat of the truck cab, a look of dark promise on his face as he shuts the door behind him. My pulse races through my body, throbbing between my legs and scattering my thoughts. I scoot along the seat, making room, but his arm goes between my waist and the backrest, wrapping around me in a smooth move. His eyes are heavy lidded, calling to me to submit to the storm in their depths. My lips part, and I trace the edge with my tongue. He's staring, and I struggle to draw breath as he pulls me in for a kiss. The taste of him is both quick and intoxicating, building on the need he's already created in me.

This isn't like any version of making out I've experienced. I hadn't realized I was craving his touch until we were flattened against each other, with his mouth taking over. I want more, more of his kiss, more of his tongue tangling with mine, and more of his body pressing into me.

"You like being here, knowing you made my dick hard." I'm speechless. Yes, I know where things may end up going, but I can't bring myself to stop him. "And knowing I'm dying to taste those stiff little nipples again." I'm both shocked and aroused, aching for his touch. I've never had a guy talk to me like this, much less touch me like this in public. Yet I want nothing more to have him take his fill.

His palm settles on the back of my waist, steadying me. Meanwhile, his other hand slips under my blouse to flip open the clasp at my back. Pushing up my bra, he sweeps over my breast with possession. I'm left pressing my thighs together to curb the wetness he's created. His thumb and index finger pluck my hard nipple, playing with the tip until the simple caress draws a whimper. Dante pulls back, his touch becoming tender as his lips move along the side of my neck, dropping kisses all the way down to my shoulder.

"I didn't mean to hurt you," he says in a low, rough voice. I don't doubt it, remembering his heated gaze when all this started.

"I'm fine," I whisper. He brings my legs up, folding them under me so I'm kneeling then pulls up my blouse. I adjust on the seat, looking around despite the tint on the windows. We're a few yards away from the sidewalk, across the road from an office building, with people going about their business. None of them aware of what we're doing in the cab of his truck.

His mouth closes around me, his tongue coming through with deep strokes around the edge of my nipple. The throbbing starts again, intensifying with every stroke. In seconds, I'm clutching the back of my seat for all I'm worth.

"That's good, baby," he murmurs, his hands at my sides. I'm practically leaning into him now, and the change in position seems to do it for him. His thumbs hook my top, pushing up until my bra is sticking up through the neckline. The warmth of his breath brushes across my breasts before his palms cover the outer curve. The heat of his mouth plays against my nipples, bringing my teeth to clamp along my bottom lip.

That's when I felt the pressure against my waist. He's slipping his hand down my belly, under the elastic of my panties to get between my legs. I should be embarrassed, knowing he'll find out I'm wet, and it's all because of him.

"Perfect." He peels down my leggings and panties, uncovering my body. I can't believe what he's doing to me...what I'm letting him do, what I'm wanting him to do. It's both shocking and exciting at the same time.

The truck's air conditioner is full blast. Cool air slaps against my butt, and everything else that's exposed. His middle finger goes over my clit then into my slit, sending a jolt through every inch of my body. With his fingers moving over my most intimate parts, I can barely think at all. I have to brace myself against a strong shoulder because nothing I've done before has prepared me for this storm.

"You're so beautiful." His voice brings me back to him. I'm so close. How could he manage that within the seconds he's had my clothes down? "Let me have your pussy," he murmurs next to my mouth as his fingers slide to my entrance.

"Ye-es," I stumble over the word, breaking it into two syllables. *God, yes.*

"Take this off," he says, pulling on the leggings.

I pull back, shoving one shoe over the heel of the other until I can drag my clothes the rest of the way off. Meanwhile, the muscles on Dante's arms are straining as he rips open a condom packet. I've rung up hundreds of them, but I never imagined this kind of heat and urgency when they'd be used. Nothing in the world can stop me from staring at his cock. Even in my limited experience, I know his size isn't typical. There's a beauty to the thick, hard flesh disappearing under the protective cover. Though he's ready, he doesn't move. Searching his face, I'm caught by the hunger in his expression, warning me he's only held back so I can look my fill—and now I'm done. Meanwhile, I'm still frozen, one leg up on the seat, one off, while I'm supposed to be settling into the back seat.

I've missed my chance. In the next breath, he's stretching out over me, his hips pushing my thighs apart as his thrust sends him deep inside me. A gasp escapes me, and I close my eyes, savoring the moment. There's nothing like the ripples from his initial entry. I can feel his possession throughout my body.

Dante hasn't moved, his heart's pounding against mine, and every muscle is straining to stay still. It's because of me—he probably thinks he's hurt me, and he couldn't be more wrong. I shift, pushing against his weight. He releases the breath he's been holding and presses his lips to my temple.

No words, from either of us. I bring my legs up around him, and he gets the idea. Bracing himself on the seat, he shifts, thrusting against me, matching the rhythm I'd even felt in my dreams.

There's never been anything better.

CHAPTER EIGHT

DANTE

With a fantastic lunch in my belly, and an unbelievable orgasm under my belt, we pull into the store parking lot. Their logo jumps out from the floor-to-ceiling window. "I hadn't realized how those eyes follow you wherever you are." I stop so a raggedy old work truck can back out of a space.

"It's my father," she says absently.

"What?" I glance over in surprise. The colorful drawing has an amazing amount of detail.

The slight hesitation tells me she's measuring her words. "Well, he didn't have the beer belly or the weathered hat, but it's still him." Her cheeks turn pink. "He caught me on a bad day, and I may have taken some liberties with his appearance."

My eyes widen. "You drew him?"

She adjusts, nearly squirming in her seat. "It started as a joke. I was getting back at him…" Her voice fades away, so I'll have to wait to find out what he'd done to earn her wrath. "One of his buddies posted a picture on social media. Another buddy shared, and the post went viral."

"Social media can make you or break you." I move up, waiting for the truck to turn.

"We were swamped. After a couple of weeks, we took on part-timers to help. Every time the buzz started to die down, I changed him, and we'd get swamped all over again."

"What do you mean, you changed him?"

"He's had several hats, the belly, a piece of grass or a toothpick in his mouth." The image is so well drawn I can picture every one of the descriptions. "Then I tried holidays."

I tilt my head in question. What the hell had she done to him for the holidays?

"You know, bunny ears at Easter." She puts two fingers behind her head. "A kiss on the cheek on Valentine's day, a box covered in Christmas decorations, overflowing with beer and T-bones." I chuckle, and her answering smile is incredible. "It was promo when we added the meat market."

"Of course."

But her smile dies away. "I should go in."

The loss weighs on me, yet she's still in the seat next to me. "Can I see you tonight?"

Her brows meet, and she looks over with regret in her eyes. "I close."

"Tomorrow?"

She shakes her head, apology in the peak of her brows. "I close all week."

Damn. Then her words come back to me. *You're going to have a long wait because I don't have a car.* "How do you get home?" I frown, knowing the answer before she can say anything.

She shrugs. "It's not far, and sometimes—"

I tighten my grip on the steering wheel, hit by a wave of resolution. "No. I'm not hearing this."

"Dante—"

"I'm picking you up." I cut her off, annoyed the fucking bastard lets her walk home in the middle of the night, by herself, in this neighborhood.

"No, you're not." Her tone turns sharp as she squares her shoulders.

I'm used to getting my way, so her wanting to argue the point leaves me stumbling into reality. Her look of determination warns me this might take a turn I won't like. However, I haven't gotten where I am by letting someone else control the situation. If I've learned anything, it's that there are easier ways to get what I want, even if I have to set things up myself.

"So, if I show up for one of the coldest drinks in town," I say, quoting the words on the fridge. "You won't let me take you home afterward?"

She purses her lips. "Uhn-uhn. Even if you're sitting out here, I'm not going to let you pick me up."

With that, she seals her fate. She just doesn't realize it.

I tighten my lips, letting her think I accept her

decision. "Fine." I lower my head in mock defeat. "You can be sure *I* won't be here tonight."

Her shoulders lose most of their stiffness. I pull her close, and she leans in then immediately pulls back, as if she suddenly remembers where we are. Her gaze goes to Conrado's car, parked two aisles away then to the sliding door. I glare at the ridiculous car as if I'm burning through the guy himself. Damn it all, I'm tempted to pull up. Because if I drive by, I'll be visible from inside, and he'll know. But that'll make things more difficult for Iris, and she's clearly rattled.

"I need to go." She unbuckles the seat belt, looking anywhere but at me. "I'm—I'm really late."

Something scrapes at my insides. There were times I'd been with a woman while she was tied to someone else. I'd had no qualms about it because the decision was hers. This time, things are different. I don't like that she's going back to him. And I don't like that I'm supposed to be some dirty little secret.

I'm not stupid enough to ignore that it's pride and jealousy that are eating me up. I feel like I'm a second stringer to *him*—and I don't consider him more than a piece of shit.

She opens the door and starts to step down. I put the gearshift in park and reach out, grasping her wrist to hold her in place. "I want to see you again." It's a statement, not a request.

"I don't know, Dante," she says, her voice full of uncertainty. She draws an unsteady breath, as if she's trying to find something to say and failing. Her gaze runs across the parking lot. "Carol's off tomorrow, and

Thursday things start picking up for the weekend."

Would I end up waiting a whole week? Anxiety tightens my chest. "Saturday, then."

She takes a deep breath. "It's our busiest night…and I…"

I want to drag her back to the seat and slam down on the gas until we're far away. I don't do any of those things. Instead, I come up with a way to keep her secret. "Tell Conrado I invited you to a party, at my place, Saturday night." I fight the bile pushing its way up my throat. "And he can be your plus one."

The fucker will likely change his tune in a heartbeat once she tells him. She'll be fine. He'll be ready to piss himself. I kiss her hard because I'll need something to hold me. I have to wait for most of the week to see her then spend the whole night figuring out a way to separate her from him.

*****

DANTE

"That's it." Kassy, my IT guru, closes the file she shared on the seventy-inch screen. It's how she joins us for these pre-event meetings, from her home in the upper northeast part of the country. Montoya calls in from the lodge. And this time Tino and I sit in the office at my place in the city.

"That's all?" Tino asks from the oversized couch. "Seemed kinda quick," he adds, pulling up the files on his iPad.

"Yeah. Only twenty-three this time," she explains, looking back at us from a secondary screen. She drags a beanie with cat ears over her long, purple-tipped hair. Why someone who's always cold would choose to move up to snow country is beyond me. "D'Santo hasn't made the transfer, and the Russian came up on FBI chatter so I nixed him."

"Is D'Santo backing out?" Montoya asks through the phone line. He prefers not to use the video function on the computer.

"It can't be a money issue," I supply, since I did the first leg of the extensive background check. "He has several offshore accounts. In fact, one of my first recommendations includes changing his banking habits. If I can find all his information, anyone can." Many times, when it comes to money, the threats come from those closest to a client.

"The guests will start arriving at the estate starting at three."

The estate. I still can't wrap my head around the term. The ranch had been home during the summer, and breaks, when I was a kid. Just a big room with a kitchen and an outhouse, up until I was about thirteen. Now, thanks to an unforeseen accident that landed Montoya on the ranch, we have room for twenty-five, plus staff, at the main house. A separate building houses the ladies who choose to entertain or participate in the auction. We bring our guests in via two private airstrips, so they won't know where they're landing.

"Iris Gloria."

Hearing her name snaps me back to attention. Her DMV photo fills the screen, younger, and with a little more weight on her. "What?" I push up in my seat, trying to grasp the strands of the conversation.

Tino adjusts on the couch, looking straight over to where I sit at my desk. Meanwhile, Kassy brings up her live feed on the big screen, scoping out the scene with more detail. "I said I ran the plates Tino sent me." She scrutinizes me as she speaks. "Tan, late model Toyota Camry registered to Iris Gloria."

The image of Iris strutting by in little more than a towel fills my head. *I don't have a car.* She just confirmed it, not more than a couple of hours ago. Didn't she? *It's not far...* I frown at the memory. I'd cut her off earlier. She hadn't actually said anything about the car this time.

"What'd I miss?" Kassy asks in a stage whisper. She's looking at Tino, expecting more details. She's not the only one wanting an explanation. Why is Conrado Villa driving around in Iris's car while she's walking home in the middle of the night? If she sold him the car, there would be a registration. Unless he hasn't transferred the title yet.

"I'm not sure," Tino answers as I'm trying to put the pieces together. "It's a recent thing. At least I think so."

I can't really blame either one of them. Nobody, least of all myself, would expect me to be hanging onto a woman.

Kassy turns back to the keyboard, hitting a couple of keys. "I can take a look—"

"No." My voice booms out with more strength than I intend.

"No," Montoya agrees. "Not yet," he adds pensively.

All three of us stare at the speaker, as if we can see Montoya, and that'll provide an answer to the cryptic remark. I don't want to know more about her. I don't want her weaknesses listed in a neat little column. If I do, I'll want to exploit them, and see how I can tear them apart to my advantage. What exactly does that say about me? And which is more important, the fact I know I'll go for the position of power or the fact I passed on the opportunity?

"So you found her," Montoya says with a certain brush of self-satisfaction.

"You knew," I counter, annoyed that he's aware of what's going on, even here.

"I couldn't be sure," he corrects. "So much in the world gets in the way when I'm trying to focus. All I can tell you is sometimes I have an overwhelming feeling something I'm thinking is right."

At moments like this, when I can feel Kassy and Tino looking my way, without actually seeing them, I understand Montoya. They're expecting the next installment of this tangled explanation, and I'll have no choice but to say I invited Iris to the house on Saturday. Why? This isn't a social occasion, it's business. Cold, hard business dealings with some of the most dangerous people in the country. Not to mention the occasional guest brought in a low flying plane, under cover of night.

Still gathering my wits, I confront the curious gazes. "Iris is…" I race to the edge of that particular cliff and stop abruptly, looking down at a dark chasm. I'm not sure how to explain who she is, much less what she is to me. I can't get the woman out of my head, but there's no clear description for that. Is there? "She's someone I met recently."

"That's it?" Kassy exclaims in astonishment. "That's all you're going to tell us?"

"There's nothing more to say." Not anything I'm willing to share. While I can go on about every inch of her body, I know very little about the woman herself.

"So how is she connected to Conrado?" Why couldn't Tino wait until later to ask?

"Who's Conrado?" Kassy asks, exasperated.

Defeated, I inhale a calming breath and set out to explain with as little detail as I can. "Conrado Villa is a small-time dealer who wants to be a transporter for our group."

Tino scoffs. "He's more of a punk."

"Yes," I agree. "A much better description."

"You know this guy?" Kassy sits forward in her chair.

Tino shrugs. "We met him Sunday night."

"You did?" Montoya's tone raises in interest.

"Can this guy even handle the type of weight our clientele manages?" Kassy asks.

"No," Tino and I answer at once.

"So then…" She looks to each of us, expectantly. "Why is he even part of the picture?"

The room gets so quiet, I can hear birds singing outside Kassy's window. Tino looks to me, as if he expects me to say something. I'm not about to tell them about my first face-to-face with Conrado. That leaves Montoya to weigh in. But the seconds tick by, and he doesn't say anything. I can feel the pressure of her question, but I stand firm.

"He holds something of great value," he delivers, as I hoped. And suddenly my shoulders feel lighter.

Kassy frowns into the monitor. "What exactly is that supposed to mean?" But Montoya says no more.

I sit back in the leather chair. "Your guess is as good as mine. I can't find anything of interest on him." I didn't try very hard, but that's not something I'll be sharing with the group. "I got word through one of our clients."

Her brow furrows. "Did he vouch for him?"

"No, and apparently he refused to acknowledge we exist. Conrado's just been making a lot of noise, exactly what we try to avoid." She scrunches her nose. "I checked, but five minutes in, I knew he wouldn't make the cut."

She immediately turns back to her desk and stops. Her fingers hover over the keyboard as my heart beats against my chest. "Can I look *him* up?"

I lift a shoulder as unobtrusively as I can manage. "Well, according to Montoya he's a potential client, so I don't see why not." Maybe she can find something I couldn't.

Her slim fingers hit the keys like automatic fire. "I found several by that name."

"His social ends in a bunch of zeros."

"Seems appropriate," Tino mumbles.

"Here 'e is." She skims the screen as my shoulders tense. "There's a whole lot of nothing." She hits a key. "Which could be something." She tilts her head, tightening her lips. "Or it could be nothing."

Tino reaches for his beer. "Whatcha got?"

"Twenty-eight. No arrests. No tax returns. No job listed. No home or apartment. No vehicle registration. No utilities. No phone."

"I told you he lives with his mother," Tino shoots through.

"Born to Olga Villa in Freer, Texas. Started school in Laredo." She hits the keyboard several times, her head dipping from one shoulder to the next as she reads under her breath. "Average student, at best." The reading continues. "Nothing of note until high school. He got called in...for stalking a girl, though they avoided using the term."

Knowing there's nothing else there, I reroute her search, considering the stalking issues Kassy dealt with in the past. "Where does he spend his time?" All I'd been able to find was intel on Iz, *Conrado's boy*, though Kassy can access infinitely more data.

"He goes across a lot." I've never been more conscious of how hard she hits the keyboard. "Uses Iris's car..." She left the words hanging, aware I messed with her search. "And a suburban registered to his mother."

"Think he's living in Nuevo Laredo?" Tino looks in my direction. Things aren't as easy to track in Mexico. With an ability to bribe or steal, people can live under the radar if they have enough to pay. "I can go over and see what I can find."

"Nah." I shake my head. Tino doesn't know it, but I already have plans for him. "He's not worth the effort."

Kassy rolls her finger over the scroll button. "From the crossing times, he lives over here but goes to visit."

"Mom?"

"Nothing on Mother's Day or Christmas."

"Check May tenth," I suggest. "Mexico has a set date for the holiday." Considering he tattooed her name across his chest, he's bound to have a solid connection to his mother.

"Checking," she mumbles, going through the list again. "No, he's actually not crossed around that date." So, how does that explain him being at the store? "Nothing much going on for Mom, either. Hang on…" Seconds drag by as she reads to herself, surely just to torture me. "She updated her driver's license last year. The address she listed is an apartment on South Louisiana Street. Two bedroom." The picture of Olga comes up on the screen. A middle-aged woman with gray-streaked hair and too many pounds on her. "She works at a tortilla factory on the same street. Her credit took a hit a few years ago, but she managed to buy the Suburban using cash."

"That's it?" Tino asks.

"Clearly not a candidate," Kassy tsks.

"You sure your mojo isn't on the fritz, Montoya?" Tino ribs.

"All I can tell you is what the universe sends me."

Kassy drops her head back on the office chair's headrest. "Well, that's a letdown."

I grin. Trust Kassy to diffuse the situation with a quick comment.

"I'm outta here. Laters." Kassy disconnects the call, cutting off Montoya also.

Tino eyes me as he shuts down his iPad. "You're not done with this."

I don't owe him an explanation, so I just say what I couldn't in front of the others. "I need you to look after Iris."

He raises a brow. "What's the problem?"

"Nothing, really," I answer honestly. "Right now it's as simple as me wanting her to get home safe at night."

He picks up the beer bottle. "Am I keeping a distance?"

"No." My grin wins out. "You're picking her up."

"I am?" He frowns, taking a quick drink.

"Yes, because I promised *I* wouldn't be there."

Tino's gaze shifts to a spot above me, his version of an eye roll. Regardless of what he thinks of my plan, he's one of the few people to "get" me.

"We'll see what happens from here to Saturday because she'll be joining us at the ranch."

CHAPTER NINE

IRIS

It's a quarter after ten when I'm finally turning off the lights, leaving the store illuminated by the sign on the dairy fridge. Exhaustion weighs me down, as if I've been doing hard labor since sunrise. Carol and I head to the door, more than ready to call it a night.

"Hey, there's a car in the parking lot," she says, pulling her backpack up on one shoulder as she cranes her neck. Tuesday and Thursday she works a split shift so she can go to college, while I try not to be jealous of her opportunity.

I shift my weight, letting my head fall back. "A regular?" Because it isn't unusual for someone to show up needing just one more thing before I lock up.

"Nah." She shakes her head, staring out the door, thoughtfully. "None of our regulars drive anything like this."

Frowning, I hurry over to the sliding door. Sure enough, when I reach the entrance, I recognize the silver BMW in the first parking space.

Carol's eyes grow huge. "Is *that* your boyfriend?"

"He's not my boyfriend," I clarify through clenched teeth.

She squees, enjoying this way too much. All I need is

for her to turn around and high-five me. "Uh-huh. But it is *him*, right? The guy from this afternoon." She grins as I set the alarm and exhale in annoyance.

We walk out the door while the alarm beeps. I pull the gate across the front windows while Dad's image mocks me from the thick glass.

"He has a *nice* car." Carol's swoony tone hits my nerves like scraping metal on metal.

But I can't deny she's right. He does have a nice car, and a damn roomy back seat in his truck. But I'm not going to bring up either one. I stick the key in the keyhole and the lock clicks into place. Glancing at the drawing again, I clench my jaw. It's long past time I change the sign. Maybe I'll try using a cute puppy, or something else with no stake in what happens in my life.

"I guess you don't need a ride after all, huh," she says in a singsong voice.

Part of me wants to say the hell with it and head to her car. It's not like Dante doesn't know better. I made it clear if he showed up, I wouldn't go home with him. But dealing with Carol will be another matter. I'm saved from saying anything by the car door opening.

My steps slow and so do Carol's. It isn't Dante coming around from the driver's side. The guy's tall, with dark hair and a similar build, but definitely not Dante. He moves around to stand beside the passenger door, his black shirt and jeans standing out against the silver car.

"Miss Iris," he says, directing his full attention at me. "My name is Tino. Dante asked me to see you safely home since *he* couldn't be here tonight."

That sneaky rat.

"I can still take you home," Carol whispers, grabbing my forearm in concern.

Tino remains impassive. His stance widens, and he crosses his hands right below his belt, the same way security people on TV shows do. Is that who he is? Dante's bodyguard? "If you prefer, I can follow you, if you planned to drive Iris home tonight."

"What the hell?" Carol exclaims, coming out of her shell in a cloak of defiance. "Why would you want to follow us?"

"Your South Side is showing," I say, under my breath.

"I. Don't. Care." She glares down at me. "You don't even know who this is."

"It really doesn't matter how Iris gets home, miss," he explains with a calm you don't normally see in people. "I just need to ensure she gets there safe."

Okay, so this is something I never thought I'd ever experience. "And if I'd been walking and refused to go with you?" I ask, more out of curiosity than anything else.

"I would drive alongside you." He tilts his head slightly. "Any other time I'd walk with you then come back, but I'm not sure about leaving the car here unattended at night."

Okay, so he has a sharp eye. I heave a sigh, knowing I can't involve Carol in anything that might become a problem. "I'll go with him, Carol."

She looks over at me, exasperated, then gives him one last glance before she juts out a hip. "Are you sure?" She studies my face, worry lines forming around her eyes.

"I'll be okay." My voice holds more assurance than I feel.

I pull my book bag over my shoulder as I walk to the car. It shouldn't surprise me Dante would find a loophole to exploit in order to get his way.

"I'm going to follow you," Carol announces, clutching her keys and waving them for all she's worth. "And I'm not afraid to call the police if I need to."

"Fine by me. In fact," he says eying her car, "why don't you lead so we don't get lost?" Clearly, he's playing to her spirit. Because if Carol has anything in spades, it's tenacity.

"I will." Carol sends him a hard glare before she approaches her little Ford. The alarm chirps, and she tosses her backpack onto the seat, following it in.

Tino opens the back door and steps aside in one fluid motion, just as I arrive.

I search the interior, making sure Dante isn't sitting there, a smug grin on his handsome face. But true to his word, he didn't show up, so I settle into the leather seat.

The door closes, and I sit here alone, at least for the few seconds it takes Tino to get around the car and into the driver's seat. How can this feel so familiar? I was only in here a few minutes, days ago. The whole situation is weird, but I'm not sure how, exactly. Is it having a driver— more likely a bodyguard—picking me up? Is having gone from nobody caring if I'm alive to having three people concerned over my safety at the same time? I don't know, but, as I inhale the familiar scent in the car, I feel special for the first time in way too long, and I like it.

*****

IRIS

In the next few minutes, I need to make sure of two things. We stay behind Carol, or she'll whip her little Ford around in a heartbeat. And we stop a block or so before the house. I don't need anyone seeing me get out of this car again and getting the wrong idea.

Tino backs out of the parking space. As I remember, the drive is so smooth you'd think we're riding on air. It's unlike any vehicle I've ever ridden in. I adjust, studying Tino's profile through the gap between the leather seats. "So how did you end up roped into this?" I ask, folding the strap on my book bag over my hand.

"No roping," he says, pulling into traffic behind Carol's Ford Focus. "Dante asked me to make sure you made it home safe."

"You don't find this odd?" I ask, though I'm not sure what I'm hoping for in an answer. If he's a bodyguard, like I think he is, then this is just another day.

"What in particular?" He glances back through the

rearview mirror. "Escorting someone home to make sure she's safe or having Dante request it?"

His manner of putting it all together leaves me wondering if I really want to know the answer. "Both?" Lightning cut through me as soon as the word left my mouth. I'm not ready to hear Dante has a habit of doing this for every woman he's run around with.

"I've been known to escort a lady home before."

Silence stretches out for another block then another. We're getting closer to home, and part of me wants to know more. Have they done this before? When did my life turn into such a soap opera? "And the other?" I ask with a churning stomach.

"Dante being involved, and especially asking me to escort anyone, is definitely odd." The whirlpool in my stomach slows down. "In fact, I would have come just to satisfy my curiosity about you."

My eyes widen in surprise. I sit forward, stretching as far as the seat belt will go. "About me?" I clutch my bag, just to do something with my hands. "Why? What exactly did he say?"

It's another heart-pounding few seconds before Tino chooses to answer. "Only that I was to see you home safely, and you'd be attending the party on Saturday."

I'm torn about the whole thing, about his high-handedness and the assumption I'll give in to whatever he wants.

"Is there a problem?" He tilts his head in question.

I couldn't help but fidget, pulling the strap around my fingers and twisting until it's as tight as my insides. "Actually, I told him I can't go, and I said not to come tonight."

A smile plays along his lips. "Dante does have a way of getting what he wants." That's not the affirmation I hoped to hear. "Yet, in a way, he still conceded." And that's no better.

"By not showing up himself?" I scoff.

"It may not seem much to you, but knowing Dante like I do, I can tell you the situation is unusual. Again, the reason for my curiosity."

Carol's brake lights flood the interior, and I have to peer outside before I realize we're home. Not a block away but alongside the darkened house, where I go in the gate. *Damn.* So much for not having the neighbors peeking between their curtains.

Tino hits the release button on his seat belt. He's about to come around to let me out. Wow. Sweet, but totally uncalled for. "I'm good." I reach for the handle. "No need to get out of the car." It's bad enough I zoned out and didn't notice we pulled up to the house. I didn't need someone helping me out of the car. "Thank you for the ride." I stretch out a leg, sliding across the seat.

"I'll be by at the same time tomorrow."

Is there anything I can say to change his mind? Doubtful. "Carol brings me home Tuesdays and Thursdays."

"Tomorrow is Wednesday," he points out.

Are all men this difficult? I close the door, careful not to slam it as I hurry over to Carol's car.

"You okay?" Carol twists around in her seat, trying to make sure I'm in one piece.

"Yes, I'm fine." I glance back and wave, but Tino isn't moving.

She puts a hand under her chin and grins. "He's waiting for you to go inside."

Is he? I glance over my shoulder at the high-end car. If it was Dante, would things have ended at curbside? "I guess I'd better go." I pull away and duck back. "Thanks for playing chaperone."

She laughs, sitting forward to buckle her seat belt. "You know, it's kinda sweet. Him looking after you and all."

"Yeah." I can't completely disagree. "But it's still weird, at least for me."

Carol stares at the steering wheel for a bit. "I don't know what to say about that."

Glad I'm not the only one.

Flipping the numbers on the combination lock, I remove the lock then push the gate open on the chain-link fence. I turn to secure it again. Neither car has moved, so I wave again, hoping this tells them I'm fine, and they can go now. Carol pulls a U-turn, ready to take off. Tino moves forward, only he stops. He's one of those people who'll wait until I'm inside to make sure I'm safe.

With an inward sigh, I unlock the door and make my way into the house. I've lived here my entire life, learned to walk along these walls, holding on to steady myself, so I don't lose a step as I move through the darkness. In my room, I hit the switch on the base of the battery-powered lantern Dad got for the boat. It's become second nature since I started using it two months ago, after the power was shut off. I still have water, but that may only last another month or two. I'll have to check the mail for the disconnect notice so I can fill the tub and anything else I can find. I want to put off dragging home heavy gallons as long as possible.

The brake lights on Tino's car dim as he moves past, while Carol takes off in the opposite direction.

Alone, finally. Now I'll have to figure out what I'm going to do about this invitation.

CHAPTER TEN

IRIS

With Carol off yesterday, one of our slower days, I've been alone with my thoughts. In fact, I've been so distracted I haven't pulled out my marketing book. Most of my day's been taken up with thoughts of Dante and his kisses. Him stretching over me in the back of the truck. Even now, two days later, I half expect him to show up again, despite having told him not to. Every time the door slides open, I can't help but look over, my heart beating in my throat. But none of the arrivals are him, and I'm starting to feel the sting of disappointment.

"Hey, you awake over there?" Carol snaps her fingers, pulling me from my daydream.

"Yeah, of course." I manage not to blush. At least not where she can see. Luckily, my back's to her. I'm at a display at the end of the aisle, stocking lime chips, one of our more popular items.

"I'm gonna grab a quick break to eat before I take off," she says, locking her till. "Looks like this might be one of those days where we get going late."

Thursdays are usually busy. You just never know if customers will start rolling in at lunch or after school lets out. But by the end of the day, both registers will have a line. Conny's due any minute, though I'm not holding my breath. Sometimes his day off lingers and he doesn't show up until Thursday night, if at all. Either way, he isn't exactly missed, so I don't say anything.

"All right, girl," I say. "Have a good one."

She pulls off her smock, folding it before tucking it in the drawer under the register. "Want me to bring you back something?" She puts up the Register Closed sign.

Even though I haven't said yes since I had the money to pay for my meal, she still asks. I'm grateful, but still, I give my usual reply, "No thanks, Carol." I'll be dining on the last hot dog in the package and week-old bread.

The door opens and I glance over, out of habit, then go back to the box I've nearly emptied. "Can you tell me where to find Iris Gloria?" the guy asks.

Carol stops, mid-step, and I'm halfway to putting some chips on the rack. "That's me," I say, eying the cap and light-blue T-shirt. Who could be looking for me?

"Delivery from *Bomberos*." He pulls up a thermal bag, setting it at the end of the packing area of Carol's register.

"Oh." I move over as the sound of thick Velcro being pulled apart echoes in my ears. He brings out a plastic bag with Bunny's café logo and places it in front of me. A smile tugs at the corner of my lips. I can only think of one person who would do this.

"And a note." He holds out a Post-it. "He sent the message for me to deliver, but all I have to write on is a Post-it pad. I hope you can understand my writing."

I brush my hands against my smock before I reach out for the yellow square, my pulse skipping a beat. *Thinking of you. Would have sent flowers but figured you'd prefer this.*

Enjoy. D. The smile stretches my lips as warmth spreads across my chest. "Thank you." I hear the cheesiness in my own voice. I can only imagine how I sound to them.

"Thank *you*," the delivery guy replies with a grin. "Your guy's a hell of a tipper." He picks up his bag and leaves while I bring the note to my chest.

"What does it say?" Carol asks, bouncing on her tiptoes. She might be more excited than I am.

Even though it wasn't Dante who put the words on the little note, I want to hide it away. It should be private. Knowing Carol, she'll never let this go, so I hand over the Post-it, reluctantly.

"Thinking. Of. You." She separates out each word, squeeing as I work the tie on the delivery bag. The scent of meaty goodness, along with something else, escapes as I pull open the bag. I take out the first plate, carefully pulling the tab loose. It's my favorite, ham and egg tacos a la Mexicana. He remembered. Again, I'm hit with a bout of cheesiness. *"Would have sent flowers,"* Carol continues. "Wow, girl, he's soooo sweet." She grabs my shoulder as she goes back to the note. *"But figured you'd prefer this."* The second plate is enchiladas, like those I picked up for Carol last time.

"I think this is for you." I hand her the plate, stopping her before she goes on.

"Whaaat?" Carol's eyes widen. "He sent something for me, too?" She takes the plate, her expression turning dreamy. "Awww. You gotta hang onto this guy, Iris."

I laugh to myself. How can I hold onto him when I don't even know where to find him?

It's a full second before I notice Olga walking around us, heading toward the back. She shows up every now and then, with no clear reason and for no particular amount of time. Of course she would choose today, at this precise moment, to make an appearance. How did we not hear the front door slide open? Maybe because we're both acting like teenage girls passing notes in the classroom.

There's no way she missed the whole episode. While she didn't acknowledge us, other than checking out the plates, she glares at me before turning her nose up as she keeps going.

"Ugh," Carol whispers. "I didn't see the wicked witch."

"Neither did I." And this will likely make hell that much hotter for me.

*****

IRIS

It took a few hours, more than she's ever spent in the store, but she finally corners me when I go to clean up.

"Conrado said you were gone when he got here on Tuesday. Where were you?" she demands, her knuckles landing on her hip.

It's been months since I left for lunch—or had a real

lunch. Usually I grab a bag of chips, or I've taken to where I'll open a pack of hot dogs and a loaf of regular bread I can keep in the back, so I have something to eat the entire week without raising suspicion. "I went out to lunch."

Narrowing her eyes, she moves into my personal space. "With who?" she shoots out. Now that's a question I hoped to avoid.

"A friend." I don't offer more because I don't really want Conny knowing he came by, much less what happened after.

She snorts. "Is that friend a man? The same one who sent you food today?"

"I don't know how that's any of your business," I snap, plopping the mop into the sink.

She pushes at my shoulder, turning me around to face her. In this light, the wrinkles around her eyes and mouth are more pronounced. When Dad went missing she fell apart, which made me doubt what I always believed about her. Though now that time's passed, things have changed. Gone is the woman who was crying and scared, gone is the woman is who sat staring at the ransom money we'd gathered, angry at the world. She's given up on him, and she's dropped the pretense of caring about me. "Don't think you can suddenly start acting like some little ho," she snaps. "You've been rolling around with a man. Don't deny it."

My nostrils flare, and my body goes rigid. How dare she say such a thing? Clearly it hasn't been important when her son is pinning me down on the desk. Conny's threat looms over me, so I bite my tongue to keep from mouthing off. I swish the mop in and out of the sink while inside I'm shaking with suppressed anger. "Even if I am, it's none of your concern, Olga."

"Don't lie to me, *pendeja*."

"Hey!" Conny shouts, as he comes through the door. "What's with all the noise?" His chest thrusts out, in that tough-guy stance he's gotten to using lately. Though there isn't enough of him to even stretch out the wife beater.

Olga juts her chin at a smug angle now that her darling son has come to the rescue. I can't let her take over the conversation because I'll end up on the wrong side of the story. So I do what I promised myself I wouldn't. Squaring my shoulders, I focus on Conny and jump in, feet first. "I was just talking to your mom about Dante coming by the store the other day and—"

"What?" He rushes over to where we're standing, nearly tripping over his own feet.

"Mijo," Olga yelps, reaching out to keep him upright. "Be careful."

His ostrich boots give an odd clump as he catches his footing. "Why didn't you tell me, you stupid bitch?" He grips my biceps, his eyes open wide with excitement. "When did he come by?"

"Tuesday, right before noon."

"Did he ask about me?"

Well he hadn't flat-out asked. "I told him you weren't here." Which is still at least a portion of the truth.

"So she *went to lunch* with him," Olga says with a self-satisfied smile. "This so-called *friend*."

He yanks his elbow from her grasp, pushing her away in the process. "I don't give a shit." The lines around her eyes deepen with her wounded expression. Then he snatches the handle out of my hand and thrusts it into hers before dragging me aside. "Here, take care of this." Olga barely grabs the handle in time, her jaw dropping as she's caught by surprise. I'm not sure what happened the past few months, but the adoration has taken a nosedive. He never would have dared that stunt six months back.

"He mentioned coming by later in the week," he says with a far-off look in his eye. "But he didn't say when it might be, and I missed him." He snaps back to attention. "What did he say?" Conny asks with all the enthusiasm of a gossiping teenage girl. "Was he mad I wasn't here?"

"He didn't say much of anything." I shrug. "We just went for a quick bite, and I brought back a plate for Carol."

He clutches my shoulder, frowning. "And?"

I exhale, resigned to the fact I'll have to tell him. "He invited me to a get-together at his place on Saturday."

He sucks in a breath, holding it for a few seconds. "Ho-ly shit." Conny's eyes go huge. "I'm in." He pulls me against him, stomping his feet. "Did you hear that, Ma? He wants me at the party."

"Well, he said you could be my plus-one," I correct. "But—"

He sets me back. "Gotta talk to Iz," he mumbles, smacking his palms to his pockets. He turns on a heel, pulling the car keys from his pocket as he heads out.

"Conrado, wait." But he doesn't slow down. "I didn't say yes." The words are enough to stop him mid-step, leaving the swinging doors half open. He stomps back inside, glaring at me with so much hatred in his eyes, his head might explode. "I didn't know this was such a big deal."

He swings around, bearing down on me with his arm raised, in a move I recognize. I instinctively shuffle away, lifting my arm up to block the blow.

"Conrado!" Surprisingly, it's Olga who stops him, putting all her weight into derailing him before he reaches me. "What's wrong with you?"

"You have until tomorrow to tell him you changed your mind." There's a steely look in his eyes I've never seen before. "If you ever expect to have a life, you'll find him," he says through bared teeth.

"I don't know how," I admit. He drags his hand up to my throat, despite Olga being latched on.

"I don't care *how* you do it," he says wild-eyed. "But you get me into that party, even if you have to suck his dick from now until Saturday. You get me?"

He wrenches his arm out of his mother's grasp before turning away. He shoves the doors open with enough force to have them slam against the wall on either side.

And how am I supposed to find Dante in time, when I told his only contact he didn't need to come by tonight?

CHAPTER ELEVEN

IRIS

I glance at the time again. It's been over six hours, and I probably checked the clock a hundred times during each one. No matter how much I wish, the hands don't go any faster.

"Let's shut it down, Carol."

"You don't have to tell me twice," she says, counting what little money is in the register. Closing out the till at the end of the day is easier now, since most people use a card.

My heart's in my throat. Will Tino be here tonight? I'd told him Carol drops me off Tuesdays and Thursdays. I go to the front entrance, searching the parking lot, but Carol's little Ford is sitting out there all alone. He isn't coming. My stomach twists into a knot. I need to get word to Dante I changed my mind about his party. If I can't, the consequences could affect the rest of my life. What if Conny flips out before I talk to Tino tomorrow night? I can only hope Conny doesn't show up. But with something this important to him, I know he will—and he might even be on time. Then I'll have to deal with whatever he dishes out, if my nerves haven't torn me apart.

I've never seen Conny raging like this. It's like he's a different person, and I wonder if whatever he's taking isn't causing the unpredictable moods. He's looking for some big score, and he's running the store into the ground, draining every cent since he got the idea in his head. We're all suffering for it, me especially. At the beginning, we could barely cover the bills. Now the produce delivery's been suspended because they haven't been paid. They're the first vendor to cut us off, and they're not the only ones we're behind with. Likely, the only reason they waited this long is because we've never been late before. Most have dealt with Dad since before I was born, and they know what's happened to him. But sympathy won't make payroll for their employees.

Despite telling Conny, time and again, he doesn't understand that once your stock goes low, your customers will stop coming. And once you sell the last item, no more money will come in. How does he expect to stay in business? How do you pay the employees? How do you pay utilities? It's all I can do to keep the place afloat and not go hungry. But if I bring it up now, he'll blow his lid, and I can't let that happen.

"Okay." Carol comes out from the storage room, swinging her backpack over her shoulder and holding my messenger bag. "I'm punched out and so ready to go."

"Thanks." Bag in hand, I head over to turn off the lights. I want to run to the door again and see if he showed up. Instead, I fight the urge and plug the code in to set the alarm. The beeping starts, ratcheting up my anxiety. Carol's waiting at her usual spot by the exit, but she doesn't mention Tino.

The door opens to the empty parking lot, and I'm both let down and stressed.

"Your driver didn't show up today?" she teases.

"No. But I told him not to come by," I reply as I pull

the gate closed and shut the lock.

"Why?" Her eyes open wide. "Did something happen yesterday?"

"No, nothing happened," I assure her. "I told him I usually hitch a ride with you."

"Oh." I swear there's disappointment in her voice.

"Only if you can, Carol. If not—"

She presses the button on her fob, disarming the car alarm. "No, it's not that." She tosses her backpack and purse in the back seat then closes the door. Sighing, she looks back at me. "I guess I got this kind of fairy-tale image about you and this guy. He seems like he cares, you know, not just wants to get in your pants."

My jaw nearly drops. I never would have expected her to say anything like that. "I suppose he *is* sweet, but I don't expect anything from Dante." Despite him already getting in my pants. "We just met."

Her head rears back. "So you don't like him?" she demands, incredulous. "I saw your face when he—"

"I didn't say that." In fact, I'm not sure what I'd say because I've been a little too into him, yet not wanting to get more involved than what I am. In a matter of days, I've learned to miss him. If circumstances were different, I would have gone out with him, regardless of what Dad thought.

"Well." She smiles, her doubts settled, at least for the moment. "You two make a cute couple."

The last word sent warmth through my chest. I liked it. I liked it a lot. Though I don't know whatever this thing between us is, it's not what Carol is imagining.

"Come on." She opens her door. "Let's go." I go around the little car, glancing toward the street one last time before settling into the passenger seat. We pull out of the parking lot with my stomach still feeling disconnected from the rest of me. When we turn off the main road, Carol glances over, a big grin spreading across her face. "Looks like he ran late."

I turn in my seat and instantly recognize the silver BMW in the side mirror. Sweet relief flows through me, leaving me weak. True to his word, Tino follows us to the house, slowing down when Carol pulls over to the curb.

"See you tomorrow," she says still grinning.

"Thanks, girl." I rush out then all but jog back to catch up to Tino.

"Everything all right?" He puts the gearshift in park, looking around with a note of concern.

"Yes." I exhale in a rush of relief. "Um." I couldn't help but fidget, pulling the strap around my fingers and twisting it until it's as tight as my insides. "I need to… Well, things changed, and I'll be able to go on Saturday after all." The relief of actually accepting out loud leaves me a bit light-headed.

He searches my face for a moment. "Good," he says, sounding as detached as usual.

"Do you have the address?" Maybe that would be enough for Conny.

"I'm scheduled to be here at eight." Annoyance wells up inside me. I made myself sick for most of the afternoon, yet Tino already counted on picking me up. "Will you be alone?"

Heat spreads up my neck and across my face. "No." I had to choke down the word. "Conny—Conrado is going with me."

"Remind him you'll be there as guests only," he adds in an ominous voice.

A sense of unease settles over me. Is this part of Conny's big score? Am I helping set up Dante? My stomach tightens again because deep down I know things won't end well if Tino has to get involved.

CHAPTER TWELVE

IRIS

It's midafternoon, and Conny's late—again. For once, I spent the day hoping he'd show up. So far that hasn't happened, even though he was supposed to be here to cover the market at noon. My nerves are starting to wear thin at this point. I don't need him getting all bent out of shape, thinking I ruined his chances at his big score. There's no telling how he'll react. As it is, lately that's getting harder and harder to predict.

Where does Dante stand with all of this? Maybe I got stupid around him the other day because at some point, in the middle of the night, I realized he didn't tell me anything about himself. Yet here I am, days later, hoping he'll walk through the door. What could I possibly do? With Carol out for class, I'm the only one at the register right now, so there'll be no surprise lunch date, no suggestions to sneak into the office for "a quick word." At this point, I'm just glad Oliver's in to cover the meat market.

"Good afternoon, ma'am." Habit adds a smile for the customer, while inside I'm hoping she can't see it's all for show.

"Hi there." The woman, whose name escapes me, starts unloading her cart, the first of the larger weekend purchases, when the door slides open again. As much as I don't want to turn, I glance over. It's Conny, finally. He's in his usual wife beater, a shirt tossed over his shoulder, but his features are strained, and he's mumbling to himself. My shoulders tighten involuntarily. *Great, he's high.*

"You're out of avocados?"

Clearing my expression, I swing back to her. "Yes, ma'am. I apologize. We're due a delivery today. The distributor's just running late."

Heading around the register area, he comes to stand beside me, his eyes shifting way too quickly.

"So, you get it done?" His hands are opening and closing as he waits because whatever's in his system won't let him be still.

"We're set for Saturday." I reach for the pack of corn tortillas as I keep ringing up the order.

"Yes! You pulled it off, Iris." He grabs me by the shoulder and biceps, shaking me in excitement. "Come on." Gripping my arm, he drags me out of the register area.

"I can't leave now." Trying to be discreet, I glance over to the lady who's just dropped another half dozen items on the conveyor belt. "We have customers," I add in a whisper.

"Damn it." Scowling, he shoves me back toward the register. Grasping the divider, I steady myself as he heads toward the office. Meanwhile, the woman folds her arms, scowling as she goes from him to me and back.

"I'm so sorry, ma'am." How many times have I told him not to be rude to customers, yet he still does this?

"All these years coming to this store," she says, shaking her head. "Tony never would have allowed this to happen."

Tears sting my eyes. "You're right, ma'am." The weight of his presence bears down on me, but I keep scanning her groceries, half afraid she'll walk away and we'll lose a significant sale. "I'll talk to Conrado in just a minute."

Even after her groceries are packed, she's still wearing a pinched expression. "Oliver," I call out to the meat market. "Can you help with a carry out?"

With both of them heading out the door I run to the back.

*****

CONRADO

Fuckin' Iris. This is important, and she's stuck on some old lady wanting groceries. I plop onto the worn office chair. I'm getting a buzz just thinking about the party. I got a plan, but as much as I hate to admit it, I can't make it work without some help. Tugging out my cell, I thumb through my contact list till I find the number I need.

After two rings, she picks up. "Mom—"

"Hi, baby. How—"

"I'm going to Dante's party on Saturday." I blow past her hello because if I don't stop that shit, she'll go on forever.

"Oh, that's wonderful."

"I gotta work something out for Iris." She's a fine piece of ass, but she's gotta put on a show if I'm gonna get the money for Dante's deal. "There's gonna be a lot of high rollers at that party. I need to polish her up to hook one willing to pay what I need."

"And you're calling me for that?" I can hear the doubt in her voice. "I thought you said you didn't need me."

I can't believe she chooses to do this now, when I have no choice but to give in. "Yeah, Mom, I need you for this."

The silence stretches out, and I hold my breath, waiting for her answer. If she bails on me, I got nobody else to turn to. Just when I'm about to lose my shit, she answers me.

"What do you need me to get for you?"

I ease my breath out as quietly as I can. "It ain't for me, Mom. I got my own shit. But for her, everything."

"Oh."

I grit my teeth at the whiny disappointment in her voice and take a deep breath. "I need to be able to show her off, in case someone wants to check out the goods."

"So something short and open at the top."

"Yeah." I pause, squeezing my eyes shut and pinching the bridge of my nose before forcing the next words out. "See that's why I...need you, Mom. You knew exactly what to do."

"Oh...well...you know I'd do anything for you, Conrado!" She giggles, and I wanna gag. Damn I hate having to suck up to people just to get something done. "I can shop faster without her. Just get me her sizes."

Before I can answer, the swinging door creaks as someone comes into the back. I spin the chair around to find Iris standing there. I check her out with a critical eye and shake my head. Calling Mom was smart. Bitch needs a serious wardrobe upgrade.

"What size shoe do you wear?"

A couple of seconds tick by before Iris raises her eyebrows. "Me?"

"Yes, *you*."

"Um, size six." Her brows draw together. "Why?"

"She wears a six shoe," I tell Mom, ignoring her question.

I can hear a pencil scratching. "Dress?"

"What size dress?"

Iris continues to stare at me.

I snap my fingers in front of her face to break her out of it. "Iiiirisss! Fuck, it's an easy question, dumb ass! Dress size?"

Iris swallows hard. "I'm not exactly sure, now that I've lost weight. It's always hard to—"

"She doesn't know," I say into the phone.

"Get something to measure her."

"What am I measuring?"

"She'll know," Mom says, blowing out a breath. "Text me the measurement. Meanwhile, I'll head to the mall. Once I have an outfit, I'll take it to a store I know that carries four-inch heels. She'll need those, they'll show off her legs and push up her ass."

"You can do that? With shoes?" Never would have thought they would help with a chick's ass.

"Yes, my silly boy."

"Okay." I exhale. Thank fuck I'm not gonna get stuck on this shopping trip. "Get whatever you think is best."

"One last thing. You're going to have to take her to the salon. I'll meet you and we can supervise their work."

"What?" The chair squeaks as I sit forward. "You're kidding."

"You want her to look good, don't you?"

I grimace, knowing this is gonna suck. "Yeah…fine. I'll take her."

"I'll set up the appointment for you."

"Okay. But make it for three o'clock because I'm not getting up early."

"You'll likely need more time. She needs a complete makeover. Hair, nails, clothes, and makeup. And it's going to cost you."

Staring at the far wall, I grit my teeth. Pretty fucking sure Dante doesn't have to deal with any of this kind of shit, but I ain't there yet. "Whatev. Get back to me when everything is set."

I jab my thumb on the screen, ending the call. Sitting back, I glare at Iris, who's got a white-knuckled grip on the doorframe. "You're gonna get shit done tomorrow."

"Wh-what do you mean?" She leans into the frame, her eyes wide and worried.

"Hair, nails, makeup—the works." I stretch out a hand, waving from her head down to the ratty tennis shoes she's wearing.

She jerks back. "I am?" she asks in an uncertain tone.

"Yeah." I tap both hands on the desk, doing a drumroll. "Need you to look good tomorrow night if I'm taking you to Dante's party." I do another run-through, trying to imagine what she's gonna look like. "That's gonna take a lot of work." That comment's guaranteed to make her tighten her ass cheeks where she's standing.

"And the store? Saturdays are usually busy."

Seriously. Selfish bitch is worried about this piece-of-shit business when my future's on the line.

"Sometimes we're crazy busy," she rattles on. "And with us barely scraping by, I don't know how we'll make it through being short two people."

"Close it up." I push up, coming around the desk as her jaw falls open.

"We've never closed the store." Her eyes are about to pop out of her head. "Not in my whole life can I remember a time where Dad closed. Even when Mom passed away, he left someone in charge."

"Some things are more important than your papa's precious store," I sneer. "Just because you fell all over yourself to make him proud doesn't mean I will." I barrel past her without a backward glance.

*****

IRIS

We've been in the air for about two hours when anxiety starts digging into me. "Are you sure this is okay?" I ask, pulling at the plunging neckline of my blouse.

"Yes," Tino assures me from the plush, leather seat across from mine. "There's no dress code for these events."

"Okay." Despite his reassurance, I still want to disappear into the cushion. The outfit Olga chose for me makes me doubt her warning about me not acting like a ho. The white, nearly transparent wraparound blouse comes together about mid-chest to show off half my breasts and outlines my nipples. Vibrant-red shorts and skyscraper heels, with what can only be described as a chrome finish, complete the look. I swear Tino's eyebrow twitched when he saw me. In that second, I wanted to run back inside and change. But for the first time ever, Conny was early, and he dragged me to the car while I tried my best to keep from spilling out.

"You'll see all manner of dress tonight," Tino assures me. "Some from around the world." Of course he thinks everything will be fine, he's in a dark suit that fits every angle of his body as if made for him.

Movie scenes of high-class parties flash through my mind, most ending with people staring at me.

"One of the more famous clients prefers silk pajamas instead of evening wear when he attends."

"Now that's what I'm talkin' 'bout." Conny laughs much too loudly. His leg has been bouncing continuously since we came onboard.

Tino turns his attention to him, sliding his gaze around, inch by inch. His ability to throw shade and look threatening at the same time is impressive. It's probably a good thing Conny is either too dense or too high to recognize any of it. "I'll remind you again you're attending as a guest, and a guest of a guest," he adds pointedly.

"Yeah, man." Conny nods, putting his neck into it. "You got it."

"No business, whatsoever, will be conducted this evening," he continues, adding a hard edge to his words. "Doing so will bring unwanted consequences."

"Okay." Conny gives two thumbs-up. "We're cool."

I bite my lip, smudging the *Scarlet Frost* lipstick the makeup artist used. If that isn't bad enough, the false lashes she put on my right eye are coming loose. At certain points, most of what I can see from that side is in shadow.

"Prepare to land." The pilot's voice comes over the speakers. I dig my fingers into the seat until my new nail tips start pulling back painfully. Normally I like to fly, but I'm anxious to see Dante again, and I don't know what Conny might be up to. I have half a mind to tell Tino to keep an eye on him, but if Conny finds out, I'll have my own set of consequences to deal with.

The plane glides in with more grace than expected. As the pilot hits the brakes, Conny's leg starts bouncing even faster, setting my nerves on edge. The smell of his cologne is stuck in my nose, overwhelming the scent of leather. It's so cloying I swear I can taste it. Tino, as usual, looks unaffected. But then he probably does this on a regular basis.

"Deploying stairs," the pilot advises. We pull out of the seat belts, and Conny hurries to the door like an overeager child.

"Damn, bro. We're in a *rancho*." Then he disappears through the doorway.

Here goes nothing. I get up a little too fast, pushing my heel down on the stilettos and catapulting myself forward. Tino's arms come around me, keeping me from hitting the floor. He steadies me, making sure I'm upright before releasing me. My face is burning. I must be redder than my lip color at this point.

"I'm sorry. I've been in running shoes for too long." Being a gentleman, he holds out an arm, walking me to the door as Conny goes pounding down the steps. He's right, though, we're out in the middle of nowhere. It's dark, but brush is growing a few feet past the SUV waiting close by.

Mesquites surround us so I figure we're still in Texas, somewhere.

"Let me go out ahead so I can help you down," he offers.

I look over his shoulder at the steep stairs. Oh, I can easily see myself stumbling down. I'm not sure if I should hope to keep my balance or break a leg so we're forced to go back to civilization.

Wetting my lips, I ask, "Think I can hold onto your shoulder as you step down?"

"Of course, if that's easier." I place my hand on a solid shoulder. If I miss a step, I doubt I'll get past him. Still, he takes the steps one at a time, letting me get my footing before moving on.

"Is this another way you'd get somebody home safe?" I chuckle nervously.

"It's definitely a first." While I can't see him, this time the smile is in his voice.

Once we're safely on the ground, he offers his arm again. His attention is on Conny, like a pit bull knowing which person is sure to cause a problem.

Leading me around to the driver's side, he opens the back door and helps me settle in. "Thank you." I hope he understands it isn't just for helping me into the vehicle.

"Buckle in." The order is unmistakable. He pulls the belt from the side and hands it to me. Closing the door, he slips in behind the wheel and speaks into his phone. "On the way."

The drive is an ordeal. Not the actual road—it's about what you'd expect from a city street, only narrower. My stomach is flip-flopping with every mile and every turn that gets us closer to Dante. Up ahead there's bright spots popping through the branches. Then the top of a house comes into view, stretching to show the length of the building as we come around the bend. The place is huge, much bigger than I imagined even with all the cars and the plane. We stop in front of the stairs, and the pit in my stomach widens. Conny jumps out while Tino steps out and opens my door in one smooth move.

"We're here," he says into his phone then tucks it into his pocket to offer his arm.

"Will you be in there…at the party?" I stumble across the question as we go around the SUV.

"Yes." He searches my face.

I glance around the back of the vehicle, slowing down so Conny can't hear. Meanwhile, Tino follows my line of sight. "Can…can you keep an eye on him?" I plead in a whisper.

His gaze shifts to me, watching out of the corner of his eyes, while he still faces forward. He barely nudges his head in acknowledgement. In fact, if I hadn't been so focused on him, I would have thought he'd just been walking.

With some of the concern off my mind, I can finally take a step without praying I won't fall on my face.

CHAPTER THIRTEEN

DANTE

I glance at the door—again. What is this, the millionth time? I know the exact moment they landed. Add to that the twenty minutes to reach the circular drive and they should be here. Yet the giant, hand-carved, wooden door, hasn't opened.

"Dante." Eric D'Santo comes up to me, scotch in hand. With his expensive haircut and tailored suit, he's every bit the well-groomed businessman I summarized in his profile. "Glad you were able to work me in." He made a last-minute deposit, and we chartered another plane so we could get him here on time. Considering the size of the D'Santo empire, even what's known to the public, it's well worth the trouble. Our people can clear up half a dozen issues to begin with, and that's just the low-hanging fruit.

"Eric, glad you could join us." We shake hands. The firm, confident grip tells me more about him than anything I pulled up on his background check. He isn't an overbearing ogre, like some, and he isn't a whiny little bitch looking for a position of dominance. In fact, he's very self-assured, as if things roll on around him without his being a part of them, and he likes it that way.

"I'm sorry for the last minute change," he apologizes. "But I had to make sure you're legitimate." He takes a drink. "I made a couple of discrete inquiries, but information on your group is hard to come by."

His words put me on alert because obviously, someone talked. "True, but then if we were easy to find, we wouldn't be effective for you, now would we." In my business, as a facilitator, I'm a very well paid go-between. People need discreet services, and we matched them with people who cater to those needs. "So, you must have excellent connections if you're able to get the information you wanted." Only people very high up in criminal society even know we exist. When it comes to vetting them, very few make the cut.

He chuckles, extending a finger away from his drink as he cocks his head. "All I got was a recommendation to accept, *if such a person exists,*" he adds.

"Excellent. I'd hate to lose a client over something so trivial." Because the contract they sign calls for the client to be cut off if it was ever known they did business through us.

My phone buzzes in my pocket. In the distance, past two groups who decided to stand in my line of sight, the door opens. I glance over, completely missing what Eric said. The tightness in my chest is back. She's here. Conrado comes in first, his red, silk shirt hanging over wide-legged jeans and the boots he's so fond of. He looks across the room as if he's found the lost city of gold.

"Some time with you later or before we leave tomorrow." Catching myself, I turn back, in time to hear some of his request. "To discuss a certain situation I need dealt with."

"Of course, Eric. Of course." Placing my palm on his arm is meant to convey reassurance. I slip, missing everything my client said. "If you'll excuse me, I have someone I have to speak to."

He glances over his shoulder, catching Iris, or the woman who's supposed to be Iris, walk in the door. We both pause. For me, there's some shock along with appreciation. She looks nothing like the woman I've come to know. Straight hair, dark brows, eye makeup, and the reddest lipstick I've ever seen. She's always dressed modestly, but today her clothing shows more than what it covers. I'm torn. While I'd enjoy being able to slip my hand into the shadow beneath her breast, I don't like that anyone else could.

"Yes, I see why you're anxious for your conversation." D'Santo gives a knowing grin. "I'll leave you to it, man." He turns on a heel and disappears into the crowd.

I can't take my eyes off her, all five foot six of my curvaceous beauty on high, high heels.

"Danteeeee." Conrado cuts in front of her, spreading his arms out, as if we'd been best buds and haven't seen each other in years. I stop, holding my drink in front of me to block off my personal space. "All right. All right." He nods, like this is all part of the plan. "Iris, come 'ere." He waves her over, making her walk around since he's rooted in place. "She's been wanting to see you."

I drink in the sight of her, getting used to the new Iris. "Dante," she says, keeping her greeting annoyingly reserved.

"Iris." I can't pull my gaze away from her, and she knows it. Her skin flushes to a pretty pink stretching down to her chest. Yes, I look. How can I not when I spent so much time enjoying her body—or thinking about it.

"She looks good, huh." Conrado's shit-eating grin makes me want to punch him. Something I won't do with everyone here. I make a quick mental note to reserve time down the road for that particular pleasure.

"Always."

"I got her all fixed up for tonight." That explains the sudden change. Still, there's no way I'm putting them in the same room tonight. I'll have to send them back to town if I'm going to get any sleep. "You like her hair like this?" He puts a hand to her shoulder, plucking a few strands. Iris subtly angles her body away from him, eying him warily while I curl my fingers into my palm to keep still.

"I like the long curls," I admit.

"You sure?" He snickers. "Maybe you need to see her from the same angle as last time." He snickers again, elbowing me as if I'm missing the joke. "You know, kinda riding low." He sets his hand out in front of his crotch. Iris loses her modest smile at the crude reminder of the night the three of us were together. My annoyance sparks a slow-burning anger as I watch her turn away, focusing on some point on the floor.

"How are we doing over here?" Montoya asks, coming to stand between me and Conrado. He's a much-needed buffer right now.

Conrado shifts away, still laughing at his own joke while the muscles in my neck are trying to pull away like cables snapping on a wire. *Patience.* Yet my palms itch to ball into a fist. I'm not doing this here, in front of everyone.

"Dante, are you going to introduce our guests?" Montoya eyes both of them as if he hasn't managed to figure out who they are. In his Armani suit, he's the picture of authority, so I play off the scene for Conrado's benefit.

"This is Conrado Villa." I send him a glare along with the introduction. Conrado reaches out a hand to Montoya, pumping it eagerly. While I would have normally dismissed his importance, Iris needs a few seconds to compose herself. She raises her head, pasting on a smile while still blinking rapidly. I admire the way she's powering through an embarrassing situation. She has a quiet strength I wouldn't have credited her with at our first meeting. "And this is Iris."

Montoya's face lights up. He's one of those people whose age you have trouble pinpointing, yet he suddenly looks younger.

"A pleasure to meet you." This time the smile is genuine. No less than what I should expect, with his harping on about a mate. He turns back to Conrado, putting a hand on his shoulder. "How about we get you a drink?"

"Yeah, man, that sounds good."

Montoya directs him away from the rest of the house, giving us a chance to escape.

Cupping her elbow, I slowly take a step back. "How about I show you around?" She perks up, readily agreeing with me for once then following without hesitation.

*****

IRIS

We tour the first floor of the enormous home together. Dante stops periodically, sharing interesting bits about the art on display or introducing me to other guests. We never touch. I don't know what I expected, but it wasn't this bit of togetherness while keeping a distance between us. Even in the middle of everyone, I feel so isolated.

"You're not enjoying yourself," Dante points out, tilting his head with a concerned frown.

"I... Um." Crossing my arms inadvertently pushes open the sides of my blouse. With a quick catch in my breath, I uncross them. My face and neck flame as I smooth out the material.

"Treacherous situation," Dante teases.

"Yes, I suppose so." My attempt at a casual smile is a miserable failure. *God, I shouldn't have come.*

"What's wrong?"

How can I tell him I don't belong here? That looking across the crowd I know I should be on the other side of the glass, looking in? Taking a breath, I answer as honestly as I can. "This is all a little overwhelming." Strong fingers fold into mine, and I finally catch my footing.

"Come with me." He pulls me around the edge of the room.

"Not so fast." His gaze rolls down to my hooker shoes then back up before he slows down. While Tino was right, I'm not the skimpiest dressed person here, the heat of embarrassment is still spreading across my face and chest. He opens a door and leads me outside. A gasp escapes me as my shoes click along the outdoor tile. The scenery is beautiful. Trees stretch out into the distance, the moon shines down on us, and the blanket of stars spreads out as far as the eye can see. I'm too busy looking up and miss his sudden stop. He's quick to catch me, pulling me into his arms. Bracing myself on his chest, I glance down to a red smudge on what has to be a very expensive dress shirt.

"Oh no." I look up at him, in wide-eyed concern. "I got lipstick on you."

"Don't care," he mutters, his arms coming around me.

The moment turns serious, and you'd think the rest of the world disappeared. "I missed you," I admit from a few inches away.

"You told me to stay away."

"Sure. You find a way around everything else b—"

Apparently the best way to shut me up is by kissing me because his move works beautifully. We're no more than a step away from each other, but I let my arms circle his neck. Yes, I'm going to be one of those people who goes from zero to horny every time he holds me close.

The warmth of his body mingles with mine. His hands are at the small of my back, covering my skin then sliding lower. One quick shift of his hips, and I realize I'm not the only one affected.

We break apart, just long enough for a breath then kiss again. Just like that I want him.

Dante pulls away. "I missed you so damn much."

I let out a harsh breath, relieved I misread him. "For a

second, I thought you might be put off."

"You didn't want to be kissed in public," he points out. "And we have a lot more people around this time." True. And though he didn't say it, I'm thinking he means Conny, too.

"Well, I hoped you'd show me an office." I glance up at him through my dense lashes. "Where I can ask you for a private word." The half smile tells me he remembers the phrase he used at the store.

"In that case, let me show you the upstairs." He puts an arm around my waist and leads me to the end of the patio. Several strategically placed stepping stones lead to the wall beneath the second-floor balcony. The last stone ends at a staircase cleverly hidden by thick ivy covering this side of the house.

After urging me on, he stops me at the first step with two firm hands on my hips. Moving behind me, he presses close, his breath whispering along my neck. The weight of his hands settles on me, his thumbs slipping inside the material, pulling my blouse open to cup my breasts.

"I've been thinking about doing this all night," he murmurs next to my ear, sending shivers down my body. His hard length is jutting against my bottom. If I wasn't wet before…

"You feel so good." It's all I can do to keep from grinding against him and taking his cock where I'm standing. I'm shocked, a little scared, and a lot excited. Never in my life would I have imagined wanting someone so much I'd be willing to be this daring.

His fingers spread around me as if he can't help

himself now that he has the freedom to touch me. My nipples are so hard, his touch sends electricity shooting through me.

"We need to get upstairs," he warns in a thick voice. "Before I end up pounding you into the handrail."

A whimper escapes me and my body begs for him to do just that, and damn the consequences.

We stumble up the rest of the stairs, my blouse hanging open. The patio light catches my attention, and I cover myself with my arm. Dante comes around me and punches numbers into a keypad to open the door. Two steps inside, and we're on each other again. He turns me around then pushes me over something solid as he comes in behind me to drag my shorts off.

I'm on his desk. *No.* My insides rebel. I can't do this. "No. Not the desk."

"Okay." He pulls back, his breath showing his effort to keep it together. "Are you—"

I stand, kissing him as I press against him until his back hits the wall. All I want is the mindlessness of being with him, of giving in to my body's needs. His hands are on my breasts again, caressing every curve as I kiss his jaw, his neck, and any part of him I can reach. Then he focuses on my nipples. Dear God. How had I gone my entire life without knowing this surge of need and pleasure?

I push the coat off his shoulders, but he takes over, brushing my breast with the fabric, causing a whole other shower of sensation. He tosses it away, maneuvering us so my back is now against the wall. I'm working the buttons on his shirt; he's dragging down my shorts, leaving me in skimpy underwear and the heels. He's much quicker than my unsteady fingers so before I can touch his chest, he takes possession of my breasts. His fingers cover every inch of my skin, pressing the outer edge to bring them together so he can give my cleavage a long, hot lick before taking a nipple. The firm tug has my body curling around him.

Gripping my leg behind the knee, he opens me wide, running his fingertips over my hypersensitive folds. My hips buck, and he works two fingers into my wet channel. My head lolls back. I'm biting my lip while he's taking his time with me. He's at my temple. "I want to take off the edge."

I clutch his shoulder, trying to keep up with him.

"Give you an orgasm before you ride my cock."

His fingers run along my inner lips, and I know I won't last long. But this isn't what I want. "If you're going to give me something"—I shift my hips—"Give me your cock." The rumble, deep in his throat tells me he likes my uninhibited demand. He lowers his chin, his hold tightening on me as if he's barely able to contain himself. I quiver as a surge of excitement shoots through me. Watching his reactions fills me with a sense of power I've never felt before. I like it.

His mouth is on mine, only this time I have a goal, so I can't let him distract me. Even when I drag free of his kiss, he's unrelenting in his pursuit, his lips at my neck. I focus on pulling open his belt, reaching down to palm his length through the expensive fabric of his pants before I go for the zipper. His heavy cock fills my palm, and I grasp him gently, relishing the fact my fingertips don't meet. I remember what it's like to take that ride with him, and I want it again—now.

A firm knock at the door brings us both crashing into reality. We're breathing hard, looking at each other to see what the other wants to do. The knock comes again, and his forehead goes to the wall. "Damn it."

I close my eyes, resigned to putting everything on pause. *Damn, why did I make him stop?*

"Come home with me." His voice is rough in my ear, but my blood runs cold. I loosen my hold on him, careful not to get too close with these nails.

"No. Conny…" How do I begin to explain? Helpless, I shake my head. "I can't."

CHAPTER FOURTEEN

DANTE

Iris slips in my grasp as my limbs lose all strength. She said no, or, more to the point, she chose Conrado. Numb, I slowly release my hand, setting her leg on the floor. Stepping back, I yank my clothes into place. This time I stare at her face, ignoring the body that had held me so enthralled. Oh yeah, despite avoiding eye contact, her body language says she knows she fucked up.

"Dante…" She licks her lips, a white-knuckled hold on her top.

Another solid knock at the door stops whatever she's about to say. Turning on a heel, I go around the desk, a strange mix of hurt and anger growing inside me with every step.

"Dante." She calls out my name again, with an edge of desperation. "Wait." Whatever she has to say, I don't want to hear it. I lift my hand to silence her without losing a step.

Wrenching open the door, I find Tino on the other side. His fixed stare and deadly calm tell me something's gone down. My stomach roils. I don't need this right now. "We have a problem," he confirms. *Of course we do.* "It's your *guest.*" The muscles along my neck and shoulder blades tense to the point of shooting pain down my back. "He was trying to work a deal outside the auction."

Why the hell did I get involved with that goddamn son

of a bitch?

A whimper comes from behind me. She heard, and she knows they're busted. Swallowing down the bitter pill of reality, I set my jaw and take stock. That's why she dragged me away. Why else the sudden interest in being with me when her last words had been *don't come back*? Maybe I should fuck her anyway, take out this anger on her. After all, it's what she was offering, a distraction fuck so Conrado could strike a deal.

Nobody has to tell me I got taken for a fool. *I know I'm a fucking idiot.* "Get her home," I spit out through clenched teeth, shaking my head in her direction.

"Dante, please..." I shoulder past him, ignoring her pleas because right now I can't even look Tino in the eye without feeling like a *pendejo*. My footfalls echo down the hall. The guests I pass have enough sense to move as I plow through, blind to those around me who aren't Conrado.

My anger expands with every step, but it should all be self-directed. I should have kept focus on the job. When had working on my future ever steered me wrong? No, it had to be a woman to screw with me. I let her drag me around by my dick, and all she wanted was to get her partner in the door. I need her gone—both of them gone from my house, from my life, and from my memory.

My nostrils flare. It should be enough I arranged for her to get home safely. As for her companion, we'll see. I might end up dumping him in the river later tonight. For now, I just need to find the asshole.

A cluster of my men move along the far wall. They're taking Conrado away from the crowd. Away from anybody who can give any sort of detail on what happened here. Good. I clench my fist because I'm going to beat that piece of crap until I can't swing my arm anymore.

"Dante." Montoya's voice comes from somewhere behind me, but I don't bother to slow down.

"Not now," I toss over my shoulder, continuing on with single-minded purpose.

Montoya hooks an arm through mine, using his body weight to change my direction mid-step.

Glaring at him, I cock an arm to let him know how I feel about getting sidelined.

"Let us discuss this for a moment." His utter calm sets my nerves on end. His gaze goes past me to the rest of the room. In my anger, I hadn't stopped to consider every guest was also a witness who didn't need to see what's happening. Giving them a show is not part of the deal, something I've never had to remind myself before tonight.

I let him lead me out to the patio, where I stood just moments before with Iris in my arms. Images flash through my mind until my head pounds. For the life of me, I can't stand here, not where I'd been with her. Maybe he could have chosen a better place, but what the hell? I took her all around the great room, showed her every piece of art on display, and I'd at least imagined kissing her in every available spot, if not more.

Montoya drapes his forearms over a nearby chair. "I see you decided to invite the infamous Conrado."

"He's a guest," I counter, trying to distract from my shame.

"Your guest was inquiring about the virgin auction, inquiring about how much a woman would fetch for her innocence…"

Fuck. That's what he'd planned to do with Iris. I sag against the wall, letting my head fall back until I can see the stars in the distance. Why had I brought *them* here? Including Conrado was a decision I made on my own, without consulting my partner, and now I owe him half the hundred-thousand-dollar door charge. Considering the piece of shit tried doing business, after he'd been instructed not to, I likely owe the entire fee. The money doesn't really matter. I have it many times over, but the reason I have to pay it does.

"I was on my way to show him out," I assure him, a migraine beating insistently behind my eyes.

"Hmmm." Any other time, Montoya's noncommittal response would have annoyed me.

The valet pulls Tino's car to the front door. Iris will be at the door, ready to be taken home. That's why he brought me outside. So she could go by quietly, and I wouldn't make a bigger scene. My chest aches, creating a hollowness I've never felt before. It unravels the knot at my throat and takes over the rest of my body without me being able to put up any resistance.

"Your lady friend," Montoya says, rather than asks.

I shove my hands into my pockets, stretching to loosen my shoulder muscles. "Iris." I don't offer more as I strain to hear the crunch of tires on the driveway, or the car door shutting with finality. A popular, upbeat song starts, and the crowd in the other room cheers, robbing me of the closure I need with unexpected desperation. She'll be gone now, or *they* both will. And I still don't know how I feel about it, which only burns even more. My shoulders slump, and I ask the question swimming around in my gut. "I'm guessing you threw Conrado in the car with her."

Montoya straightens, brushing some invisible dust off the sleeve of his designer suit. "No," he replies, casually folding his arms. "I invited him to enjoy the harem."

"What?" Every muscle goes rigid again, shooting tension down my back and behind my eyes. I glare at my partner, wanting to rip his neck out. "What the fuck are you doing?" I ask straight out because trying to read him will get me the same answers as always—a big lot of absolutely nothing.

Montoya cocks his head, the light spilling from the house, catching the white strands in his hair. "I don't know yet."

I scoff, a shot of mad laughter escaping as I shake my head in disbelief. "The guy…is a *miserable* piece of—"

"It's not him I'm interested in," Montoya cuts in. "Conrado himself is of no consequence. It's what *he holds* that will be valuable in the end."

Experience tells me I shouldn't bother asking how he knows. Because he won't have an answer. Instead, I stare out into the distance, catching a glimpse of taillights between the branches. I stand frozen, watching as they disappear into the pitch black covering all the mesquite and bramble surrounding the lodge. I keep my attention there, mostly because the urge to pound my fists into something is growing stronger, and Montoya would be the only target in reach. I fucked up enough already, I don't need to add any more random acts of stupidity to the night.

"Trust me, Dante," he assures me, putting a calming hand on my arm.

I shake my head, letting some of the tension drain away. What can I possibly say? My head is filled with the fact she betrayed me, and *I let her.*

"I have to get the hell out of here." I spin around, leaving him, and a house full of guests I personally vetted, without a second thought.

*****

IRIS

"Are you okay?" Tino keeps asking, but I don't know how to answer. A yes would be a lie, and a no might just make me fall apart where I sit. So I cradle my arm and keep my fingertips against my lips, fighting the urge to bite these gaudy nails as anxiety washes through me.

The blanket of city lights in the distance is beautiful. It's been years since I've been out of Laredo, even if this was just an outing to a ranch. The place is majestic, at least what I got to see. Is it his place or Mr. Montoya's? Maybe both? The older gentleman has an unmistakable air of authority. I may never know now.

I bite my lip to stop the trembling. He'd been so enthusiastic while he showed me around. My eyes burn, making me blink back the tears trying to escape. Why had I been so selfish? Why didn't I follow him through the rest of the house? Maybe if I hadn't practically jumped him as soon as I had the chance, we'd be having drinks right now instead of...having Tino drive me home.

I need to get my mind away from what happened with Dante. I should worry about what happened to Conny. It would be too much to hope he would just disappear, and I'd never have to worry about him again. With my luck, all he'll get is kicked to the curb, and somehow that will be my fault.

"What did he do?" My voice comes out as a croak.

"He broke the rules." The ominous explanation doesn't surprise me at all, but it still doesn't give me the answer to the only relevant question.

I sit back in the car's plush seat, unseeing. So what should I expect now? As usual, Conny didn't listen to what he was told. He ignored Tino's instructions, despite him going over them several times before we got to the estate. What would I have to deal with tomorrow? Or maybe the day after, because likely he wouldn't be in to work on Sunday. Not after taking off to God knows where and a dummy flight just to end up an hour or two outside of town. It's all a fake-out, a lie so people don't know where they are. Why? Because they're up to something against the law. Yes, deep inside I knew, I just chose to ignore it.

Minutes later we're back in town, the lights going by in a blur as we take the loop.

How can I tell him what happened? Conny is ready to turn me in at a moment's notice. I'll likely spend time in jail over something I didn't do. Images flash through my mind, like the eternal second when you think your life's coming to an end. My mother, thin and frail, being sick in a narrow, blue bucket. My father and I having a meal together at Bunny's. Olga. The store. How much I wanted to go to school, to break away from my father's expectations. It's gone now—all of it. Yet none of that compares to the way I feel right now. Raw and ragged, as if I took a beating, not physical, but a long, drawn-out emotional one.

How did Dante become such a big part of my life so quickly? I constantly tried to distance myself from him—from men in general. They'd never been there for me, or my mom, when we needed them most. Not even my own father. So how could I expect Dante, someone I met a week ago, to be any different? My nearest and dearest example had shattered with my parents' marriage. They included my mother dying practically alone, while the man who'd sworn to love her in front of God and family was in the guest room asleep, next to his girlfriend. A woman who had been ready to throw out my mother's things by the time we got back from the burial. The topper was the huge fight only hours later because she wanted to move into the master bedroom. That's when I really saw her for the first time, without the phony friendship and concern.

I'm dumb to think things were different. Always seeing what I want instead of what's actually there. What would this be to him? A quick hookup? And I've been foolish enough to miss him so much I'd been about to give myself to him without a second thought, only to have him turn on me.

The door opens next to me. We're in front of the house, and Tino's standing by the door, his brows scrunched in a mask of concern. When did we get here? How long have I been lost in my own thoughts? I look around for my book bag, briefly forgetting we weren't coming from the store like every other night. Heat runs up my cheeks as I step out of the car, taking, and actually needing, the hand he offered for support. Stress weighs down my legs, my entire body, making it a chore to drag myself out of the seat.

"Will you be okay, Iris?"

It's more words than he's ever said to me on his own. Though I heard the question many times, I still don't know what to say. Holding my head high, I force out an answer. "I'll be fine." Hopefully that'll be enough to let him leave in peace. I step forward, making my way up the driveway to the gate, teetering on the whorish heels Conny chose for me. Flipping the lock up, I turn my thumb sideways, fumbling over the tumblers with these ridiculous nails. Somehow, I make it inside without bothering to look back at Tino, though he has no fault in any of this. But when I make it into my room, I don't bother turning on the lamp. I toss myself facedown on the narrow bed and do the one thing I haven't done in months. I let myself cry, feeling sorry for the girl I'd been and the woman I'll never have the chance to be.

CHAPTER FIFTEEN

DANTE

I spent the longest days of my life at the house I grew up in. Two small rooms still sitting at the back of the ranch. My father picked the location because the ground is too sandy to plant, so he didn't waste valuable land. The house is close to the river. As a kid, I'd try to catch a good wind so I could flick bottle caps into the water.

It's the first place I thought to go. I needed to be alone, surrounded by overgrown mesquites, an outhouse, and a handful of creatures that can kill me. Turns out, no matter how far you run, you still long for what you want. Close enough to want to reach out and close your hand around the thing that burned you the most.

With nothing stronger on hand, I head to the nearby well my father and grandpa dug before I was born. Grabbing the metal bucket off the peg, the handle squeaking in protest, I drop it in. The bucket lands with a splash, sinking deep and filling to the top. Grasping the rope, I pull back, a few feet at a time, welcoming the weight to help me burn away my stupidity. Though nobody in their right mind would want to touch water from the Rio Grande, the dirt and sand on this part of the ranch filter out the impurities, leaving everything clean enough to consume. A scoff escapes me. Funny how things can come out lily white when you least expect it.

Her face comes into focus, her expression pleading for understanding. *I can't...*

The phrase goes through my head for the millionth time. Why would I assume she would leave Conrado? I'm still baffled. How could she choose him after he offered her up in public, for fuck's sake? She'd been embarrassed as hell, yet she'd kept her mouth shut.

He even dressed her with an eye to undress her easily. How many more men had he planned to offer her to? My head fills with an image of him pulling back her top to show off a perfect breast to anyone willing to shell out the cash. My stomach tightens, and my anger flares up again. *Goddamn that son of a bitch.*

Cupping my hands, I plunge them into the bucket, bringing water up to splash my face. Then there she is again, coming out of the motel bathroom in a towel. Two more handfuls don't erase the image from my mind. I don't know if anything can.

In a fit of annoyance, I grab the bucket, bend at the waist, and dump it all over my head. Straightening, I send a virtual river down my back and chest into my pants. Hell, maybe that's what I need, to dunk my dick in cold water. That should be enough to cool me down. The snort is a surprise, even to me.

Putting the bucket on the hook, I head back to the house, my toes squishing in my shoes. I spent way too much on these damn things to have them hauling water, but what the hell. I stop at the doorway, the bare walls of my childhood home glaring at me in accusation. My family would have welcomed the money I used on shoes to keep the occupants fed for months on their meager rations. It's hard to imagine I grew up out here, but I did.

I take a deep breath and lean on the doorframe, shoulders sagging in defeat. I've let my success push me too far over the edge. I expect everyone to do what I want, when I want, even if I have to find a way to make it happen.

Hell, I chose not to pry into Iris's life. I wanted her to be different, and the mistake cost me. She must have her reasons for wanting to stay with Conrado, reasons I don't want to think about right now. Losing her hurt, and I hadn't felt anything for anyone in way too long. The fact she'd been so different from the others made her special.

Any other guy would have picked up the pieces and gone back to his life by now. It's time I head to town and deal with my shit. A hot shower and a good meal will carry me a long way toward normal. Then I can decide what to do next. Maybe I'll buy a yacht and get away for a while. Only I'll go to the West Coast because two hundred miles isn't nearly far enough away from the temptation to find her.

*****

CONRADO

Click-click-click-click-click. The dial on the safe goes flying around. Once it stops, I put three fingers over the knob and move it slowly. It gives me a rush, thinking about the payout as the white line on number eleven hits the marker. I turn the handle for that final snap and pull back the door.

Stacks of bills, wrapped in different-size rubber bands, sit there waiting for me. They're not smooth and flat, like I expect. These bills have been around, so the ends stick up, making the bundle look bigger.

"Duuuude," Iz says from behind me.

I reach in and grab two handfuls, pulling them out. I'm fuckin' rich. A stallion—no, a bull. One of those big motherfuckers that throws the rider. "Whoop-whoop." I bring one hand to my lips and drop a loud smack then do the same with the other before I drop the money on the desk and go back for more. It took forever, but I nearly got what I need for the deal.

"Dude, you sure we got enough?" Iz leans forward.

Man, he always has to be the fuckin' downer. I toss the last of the bills on the desk and frown. Every single time…and he wonders why I don't bring 'im along when I'm trying to deal.

"Don't worry, man." I wave him off. "We're close then we hit easy street."

I like how Dante and those dudes roll. Private jet. Escalades. His guys at the door, checking out the guests coming in for the party. That's what I want, a big fuckin' house that's mine. *Mi cantón.* And a bitch in every room. Maybe I'll find the ones from my favorite porn site. I can't help but grin because I know this deal with Dante would make it happen. It's stupid money.

"These people are talking millions. Millions."

"Fuck, dude." Iz throws his hands up in the air. "If you'd closed the deal for this chick…"

"I know, man." I stomp a boot down and hold up a thumb and index finger. "I was this close. This close."

The way the shit went down wasn't my fault. I'd set it up perfectly. If Iris had done what she was supposed to do, I'd be making big plans right now instead of sitting in this shitty little office. But no, even with her tits out, she couldn't hold his attention. I scoff. Maybe she ain't classy enough to someone like Dante.

Lucky I worked a backup plan, giving the guy at the party my digits. Maybe the guy at the party will still call for her. I bet I could get more outta that fat bastard. Then I'd have a chance to do this without getting into more of the money from my other deal. He's gotta know finding a virgin ain't easy. Especially for a guy like him. That's *if* he calls.

Sometimes it feels like life and everyone in it just fucks me over. I got nobody on my side. Nobody wants me to do good. Not even my mom and for sure not that bitch Iris. Dante's the biggest player in town, and he passes on her? Shit makes no sense. It's like she did it on purpose.

Wait... *Did* she do it on purpose? I think back to the other night. His guys cut me off real quick. I shoulda stayed with Dante, and I woulda met the right people. As it was, I barely got to give the guy my number. Hell, how was I supposed to know we couldn't work something out on the floor? I was Dante's guest. Damn, did she set me up? Best I find out right now and, if she did, she's gonna pay with everything she's got.

"You know what?" I look up at Iz, who's still staring at the stacks of money with lust in his eyes. "Get Iris the fuck in here."

*****

IRIS

"Hey, Iris!" Iz, Conny's sidekick, waves me over toward the stockroom. "Rad's calling."

I give Iz a thumbs-up. Both he and Conny thought the nicknames they'd come up with made them sound tough. But to me, "Conny" would always be followed by "girlie-man," in Dad's parody of Schwarzenegger's accent. A smile plays at my lips as I lock the till. "Be back," I say to Carol as I head up the aisle, past the *Employees Only* sign to the darkened area. The only light comes from the office, where Conny's pacing, just inside the doorway. The hair on the back of my neck stands on end, so I take the last few steps slowly, glancing into the dark corners with heightened awareness.

"You..." I wipe my palms on my jeans, trying to push past the knot in my throat. "You were looking for me."

Conny stops at the edge of the desk. "Get your ass in here." He does that hand-waving thing he likes to do, but the stiff angle of his shoulders screams for me to keep away. I take a couple of steps but stay as close to the doorway as I can.

"I know what you did," Conny sneers, his eyes glassy, and his mouth twisting with every word.

Great, he's high and he's pissed. And from the sound of it, I'm the reason. Fear shoots through me like an ice storm, freezing my brain. What can I say to help settle him down? How had he found out about what happened in the motel, or the truck? Had Dante told him? I shift my weight then take a half step back, just in case. A pair of clammy hands clamps around my arms. I crane my neck around to find Ismael standing behind me. "Hey again." He grins, jutting out his chin.

This asshole is the reason Conny's pissed off. He probably egged him on about the big-brother crap. Not that Conny's ever truly been any kind of brother or protector.

"You *think*," Conny continues on his train of thought, "because Dante invited you to his place, you're all that." He looks me up and down, his nose wrinkling in distaste. "And I'm supposed to be *your guest*. Me." His nostrils flare. "I'm supposed to be fucking grateful you'll take me?"

"No." I shake my head in confusion. "I don't." What lies has Ismael been feeding him?

Conny blinks hard, like he is trying to focus. "Don't. Lie. To. Me."

"I didn't ask to be invited," I assure him. "You wanted to go."

Conny's hand shoots out, catching me across the jaw. "Stupid bitch. I don't need you. And he…" In his current mood, words escape him. My stomach twists so hard I'm afraid I'll puke. No matter what, this isn't going to end well. "He don't need no hood rat like you to suck his dick."

"I didn't—" His hand catches me again. Pain blankets the side of my face. Blinking back tears, I do my best to stay still because having him chase after me will only make things worse.

"Dante," Conny spits out, jabbing his finger in the general direction of the front door, like Dante's waiting outside, "has a house full of *putas* like you. Better than you." He points his finger at me. "He can fuck a different one every night."

Anger comes bubbling up from deep inside. "I'm *not* a *puta*." The words are out before I can bite them back.

"*Puta*," he shoots back, his voice dripping with distaste.

"Anything I am," I yell, "you made me." What little I messed around with my boyfriends had never gone beyond light petting. I'd always thought one day Dad would walk me down the aisle, and I had to deserve to wear the white dress Mama wore. Now I'd lost both of them. The thought I'd locked tight in my heart finally broke through. Tears escape, and I let bitterness and anger spike my voice. "What you and *your miserable excuse for a mother* did to me." Though I may later regret it, I said it because it's true. And mostly because I know it'll hurt him.

It did. And I enjoy the stark fury in his expression for a fraction of a second. Then he shoves his fingers into my hair and grips my scalp. Wrenching me forward, he slams me down on the desk. My teeth bite into the inside of my cheek as my face flattens against the wooden top. I howl in pain, but I have no one but myself to blame for pushing his buttons.

"*Puta*."

My shoulders tighten. The coppery taste of blood coats

the side of my mouth.

"You ain't nothing to a guy like Dante."

He leans down next to me. "If you ruin this for me…" he threatens, spittle speckling the side of my face.

"I won't help you screw Dante over." Regardless of how things ended, I can't be part of what he's trying to do to Dante.

"I don't *need* your help. Everything I need is right here." His hand comes down hard on my right cheek, and he squeezes until his fingers dig painfully into the curve of my bottom. "I'm going to hand you out to any *pendejo* willing to pay a dollar for your ass until I have the 50K I need." Ismael is standing at the doorway, laughing out loud at Conrado's threat.

He would probably be the first one to step up because, like Conny, he's always looked at me in a way that made me feel dirty.

"How about a little taste of this," he says, rubbing his hand over his crotch.

"Yo, you can have her ass, bro." His fingers slide between my legs while I squirm to get away. "This pussy, is all mine." He pulls on my jeans, which move down way too easily since I lost weight.

"No." I struggle to push up, but he anchors his hand at the back of my neck.

"You have no idea how much they pay for a cherry like this," he says, as if it's a normal conversation. "Especially on someone who looks like her." I keep trying to pull up my jeans, but the air-conditioning hits my bare bottom, and I know what's going to happen, again. Only now it's two of them.

"No," I sob, pushing to get up off the desk. The door squeaks. Is someone coming in, or had Ismael moved from the entrance? I want to die just knowing Carol or Oliver will find me like this.

"Yeah, she's prime, dude."

"What's going on here? Conrado!" It's Olga, and I've never been so happy to hear her voice. "Ismael, you get yourself out of here," she scolds, her voice harsh. "You let that girl go." Conny's hand comes off my neck, and I nearly sag in relief. "What's wrong with you? The door is wide open, and there's customers up front." I get up off the desk, clutching at my jeans and stumble away. Shoving Ismael, I run past him to the bathroom, where I can lock myself in.

I need to calm down before I can face anyone.

CHAPTER SIXTEEN

DANTE

Just when I thought I might be able to sneak in for some comfort food, I find Bunny putting a Help Wanted sign in the front window. She looks up, straight into my face, so it's impossible for me to keep going when I'm grasping the handle. She winks, waving as I push through the glass door.

"Well hey there, handsome. Didn't expect to see you back so soon," Bunny says, with a level of enthusiasm I'm still not used to. She cranes her neck, trying to look behind me. "Is Iris with you?"

After years of conditioning, I don't react, even though she's tugging at my guts.

"No." I shake my head slowly. Why didn't I keep walking when I had the chance? "Things didn't work out."

Her head jerks back in surprise. "You dumped her?" The accusation in her voice cuts deep, maybe because she's someone close to Iris.

"No, actually I wasn't the one to decide." Maybe that would be enough to set her straight. But the way her expression hardens reminds me of Tino, so we're nowhere near done.

She pulls back, tilting her head and folding her arms. "Did you try to push her into something she didn't want to do?"

Now there's a loaded question. Things hadn't been that simple, so I borrowed from what Iris once said to me. "Things were complicated." Yet I braced myself for more because she asks questions matter-of-factly and with no regard to privacy. As if a dozen people aren't hanging on her every word, wondering if I'm some deviant.

She unfolds her arms, her expression relaxing. "Yeah well, such is life." With a quick exhale, she goes around the counter, tapping at a spot where I can sit. "What can I get you?"

"Chile relleno." Every step is like trudging through high water. I pull out the weathered log stool, ignoring the people I can feel watching me. "To go." Because I'm not going to sit through another round with a female version of Tino wanting to interrogate me.

"You got it." She hustles over to the kitchen entrance and pushes the door open to shout my order before stepping back. "Coke?"

"Sure." Pouring it might focus her attention somewhere else. But when she brings the drink, she lingers. The best I can do is settle on a neutral smile.

"You're not working the kitchen?" Hopefully this will sideline the next round of the interrogation.

"Not today." She grabs a towel, wiping down the counter, though the area is spotless. "Had to let a couple of people go." She exhales, twisting the corner of her lips. "One of them was the cashier, and she's family," she adds, shaking her head. "It's getting to where you don't know who to trust anymore."

It's the one thing my clients complain about most. They can't find someone to trust, either for themselves or with their money.

"Don't be too hard on Iris." Bunny's voice is low and thoughtful. "Little sister's had a hard life."

The flyer with her father's picture jumps out at me. "Yeah, I guess she has."

Bunny keeps one hand on the counter, twisting her torso to look back. "That's not the worst of it."

I switch back, giving her my full attention.

She tilts her head in a slow move. "In fact, having him gone might be a blessing in disguise."

The statement is so unexpected, the corners of my mouth drop.

A fork clatters on a plate. "I heard that," a man snaps from the back of the room.

With a quick swivel, I catch a short, barrel-chested, man pushing away from a table at the back.

"Cappy," Bunny calls out, waving him over. By her cheerful tone, I assume the older guy's a regular.

He draws a napkin over his mouth. "It's not right to speak ill of the dead, young lady." His craggy voice, evidence of a longtime smoker, belts across the room. His steps are slow, his left heel dragging as he comes closer.

"Cappy, this is Dante, a friend of Iris."

"Dante," he says, with a critical eye on me.

"Sir." I hold his gaze, letting him know I'm not intimidated.

"Cappy's a friend of Iris's dad," she explains, before turning back to him. "And you don't know he's dead," she points out, setting a hand on her hip.

He looks her in the eye, planting his feet as if getting ready for a fight. "We both know people don't come back from there, not after this long."

She releases an exasperated breath. "Isn't he supposed to be your buddy?"

"Doesn't make what I said any less true."

She leans her weight against the counter, giving me her full attention. "You know my mom and Ellie, Iris's mom, were besties."

"Yes." Iris had mentioned it at one point.

"We lived across the street for most of my life. Mom broke down when she heard about Ellie's diagnosis. Cancer." She winces, and I join her. "With her dad out of the picture, Iris took care of her mom. She was sick through most of Iris's high school years. Poor kid, sometimes she looked ready to drop. In the end, it took her an extra year to get her diploma."

That explained at least one big question. Taking care of a sick person is hard enough, but trying to be a caretaker while going to school would be rough. It left Iris no time for a life of her own.

"Then she couldn't go off to school, thanks to her dad," she adds as a jab.

"Hold on there." Cappy holds up a hand. "Tony wanted to make sure she was around for her ma."

"And how is that fair to Iris?" she snaps back.

Cappy shakes his head, pointing at his hair. "When you have this much gray hair, and a couple of kids to give it to you, you'll understand." Her glare doesn't slow him down at all. "We all lost our kids," he explains, pointing a thumb over his shoulder at the other three at his table. "They gone off to college and never come back, other than the holidays, or when they need money. Tony just didn't want to lose his little girl."

"He kept her at the store, day and night, as soon as her mom got better," Bunny explained. "How is that 'being around for her ma'?"

"Ellie getting sick was a reality check. He wanted the girl to learn how to run the store while he could still show her. He wanted her to be independent, not have to depend on someone else to pay the bills." His expression said he'd never expected her not to realize Tony's plan. Despite good intentions, Iris got a raw deal in life.

"More like, run the store for free," Bunny shot back, tensing so much the well-defined arm muscles rippled.

"Nah." Cappy shakes his head. "He put away money for her education. It's in a separate account because he didn't want Olga getting her hands on it."

"That no good piece of crap." Bunny scrunches her nose, as if she's smelling something rotten. "She had the balls to push her way into the house, staying there with Tony. And *he* let her!"

"So he still lived at home?" The question popped out because I can't believe the guy would take his girlfriend to live with his wife. Did he give a shit on any level?

"No," Cappy said defensively. "Well, not till Ellie got sick again."

Shit. And I thought things couldn't get worse. Bunny caught my surprise. She presses her lips together.

"Yeah, they went through the whole thing all over again," she confirms, her voice thickening. "Only the second round was too much for Ellie's body, and she didn't make it."

A guy brought out my order, leaving the plate beside Bunny. She didn't offer it, and I didn't ask. I'm still trying to process the situation. The drama in that house must have been unimaginable.

"Mom hhhhates her. Capital H," she adds, spreading her hands wide to emphasize how much. "She says Olga's a piece of work. Raunchy bitch would have humped Tony in front of his dying wife, just to stake a claim." Wow, the woman they described didn't fit the picture Kassy pulled up.

"Yeah, it sounds like something she would try." Cappy shoved his hands into his pockets. "Tony moving back was supposed to be a clean break from her."

"Oh?" Bunny's eyebrows shoot up. "Did Olga know, because she asked me about catering their wedding." She sniffs in disdain. "I told her I'm too short-staffed to be doing catering."

Cappy shook his head. "It wasn't ever gonna happen.

He never divorced Ellie."

Bunny's eyebrows shot up again. "Didn't know that."

"Weeeeell, they had their problems." He shifted as if uncomfortable with this part. "But he still loved her. He was just stupid and got caught," he adds, as if it explains everything. "Tony supported his wife and kid, and kept both on the insurance." He gave a humorless laugh. "Drove Olga crazy." Which seemed to be a plus for him. "She was pissed because she and that worthless kid of hers lived in an apartment while Tony's daughter and wife kept the house."

Now that catches my attention.

Cappy grins. "Tony took his kid to learn the business. He took her kid because he was a lazy son of a bitch and needed to learn how to work."

A hollow feeling crawls up my throat and settles in.

"Never did like her kid," Cappy clears his throat. "Always spent too much time staring at Iris in some weird, pervert kind of way."

Yeah, but he must have done something right because she'd chosen to stay with him instead of me. Even so, in the back of my mind lingers a nagging suspicion that I was missing something.

*****

IRIS

It's been four days, yet when I close the gate in front of the store, Tino's waiting patiently in the parking lot. He pulls up to the entrance since the rain's coming down hard. By now, he knows he doesn't need to get out of the car. I can open my own door. He's doing more than enough to be out here waiting on me at ten o'clock at night, in a storm. I've slept in the warehouse before to avoid the weather. I could have done so again.

"Good evening." His voice is as neutral as always.

"Hello." The last six hours weighs on me, and you can probably hear it in my voice. Tino pulls away from the entrance, but his gaze lingers. He realizes something's up, but he doesn't ask. For once, I'm glad he's the silent type. Though his silence is driving me nuts. Why doesn't he say something about Dante? At this point, even an accusation would be welcome, so I can explain I'm not part of Conny's plan. Why did Dante tell me about the thing on Saturday? If I didn't know, I couldn't tell Conny. Instead, I foolishly let my temper get the best of me and blurted everything out.

The blocks roll by. He's taking a different route today. The one I always use when I walk, so I can avoid traffic and the guys sitting outside their house, quietly exchanging drugs for money. The pressure to find out more, to explain and shake the weight of guilt, forces me to speak up, because this may be my one shot at fixing things.

"Dante...still has you coming by?" I ask, barely hearing my own voice over the slap of rain on the car roof.

"He never told me to stop, so I didn't." Eagle eyes linger on me from the rearview mirror. While what happened earlier shouldn't matter to him, I turn, looking outside so he doesn't see the bruise forming on my cheek. This isn't part of what Dante told him to do. Besides, why should I expect him to care now? He thinks I set up his friend or boss, I'm still not sure which.

"He hasn't asked about me?" My voice sounds pitiful to my own ears.

Tino drives on for a block without answering. Part of me wants to take back the question, pretend I never said anything. The other part of me wants answers, though I won't be around for whatever happens.

"He's not in town." The words are stiff, isolated.

"Oh." Nothing else comes with his curt explanation. The loss tears through me, burning my throat and the back of my eyes. I suppose I held onto a shred of hope things could work out. Stupid but true. This seems to be the norm for me now.

The car stops, and this time I recognize I'm in front of the house.

"Tino." My voice is stronger this time. "Thank you for everything, really…but don't come back." I open the door and step out, heading to the gate without looking back. True to form, Tino doesn't drive away until I make it through the front door, even though my fingers are numb and I'm fumbling with the key.

I stumble inside, soaked through, and collapse against the sturdy kitchen door. Thunder cracks overhead as the storm unleashes its fury. Lightning cuts through the darkness surrounding me, momentarily illuminating all the things familiar to me before plunging me back into darkness. What am I going to do? I can't live with what Conny threatened. I won't. I'll choose death rather than end up passed around from man to man until there's nothing left of me. My only other option will likely send me to jail, and who knows how many lowlife friends Conny has in there. Which is worse? I don't honestly know how bad this could be, and what else they may have done I'm unaware of.

Conny is running the store into the ground. We're down to two employees, and he's barely leaving enough to pay them, much less the utilities. We're going under, and I can't do anything about it.

Anxiety rushes through me like a wave, setting my head to pounding. I'm reminded of when Dante first came into the store. My eyes sting again. Why hadn't I kept my mouth shut? He could've gone in and out without ever noticing me. Tears begin to overflow. This thing between us is over, and my heart's crumbling at the realization. Maybe, somewhere inside me, I held out hope he's cooling down. That in a day or so he'd want to talk to me, even if he just wanted answers. How can I try to figure out what he's thinking, when I know very little about the man himself? And that's limited to what it's like to be with him and how he makes me feel.

I have to make a decision. Should I go to the police? The images Conny's holding show me taking money from the safe. While I can explain we were waiting for a possible ransom, the call never came. Where's the money? And where is my dad? We'd had a very public argument before he disappeared. I look guilty, though I would never physically hurt my own father. But when you've actually yelled at him, saying you'd wished he'd been the one to die instead of your mother…well, there's nothing in the world you can say to change that.

My legs go weak, and I slide down the door into rainwater puddling on the floor. I've lived with this agony too long, with a threat hanging over me, choking me, leaving me wondering about my future. I know what I have to do, even if tonight may be my last night of freedom.

CHAPTER SEVENTEEN

DANTE

Distant lightning forks across the sky as I pull up to the tarmac on the ranch. My cell rings, lighting up on the passenger's seat. Snatching it up, I find Tino's name across the top of the screen. What could he want? I leave my thumb hovering over the home button, unable to press down. My heartbeat echoes in my chest. He must be heading home after dropping her off. So, why is he calling? And why did my pulse kick up when her image filled my mind?

The phone rings again, forcing me to answer. "She asked about you." Tino's voice comes from far away, yet the note of urgency puts me on edge.

"Iris?" My pulse is beating against my throat now.

"You're a lot of things, Dante. Stupid isn't one of them," Tino adds in his deadpan voice.

If there's anyone who will call me on my shit, it's him. The reason I left the city was so I didn't go find her, especially after Bunny brought her to mind. And I didn't want to be home, waiting on him to tell me he was back from dropping her off. Or worse, not say anything at all. Though I didn't ask, I know he's still picking her up every day. I don't want to end up telling him to stop because the man I'd become would do so.

"What happened?"

"Something's wrong." The note of confusion in his voice makes me frown. "But I don't know what."

"What?" For once, I can truly appreciate his regular, on-point comments.

"It's weird…" He blows out a breath. "Like Montoya-shit weird, man."

"But she was safe when you left?" Thunder rolls across the distance, getting closer.

"Yes."

The tension in my shoulders relaxes a little. "So your spider sense is telling you?"

"Shut the hell up," he barks. For a guy whose life's been spared more than once due to some heightened ability to sense danger, he really fights it. "She told me not to come back." Something in my chest collapses with the reality of his words. "But it's how she said it that bothers me. She sounded so defeated." I can't imagine her without the brightness in her eyes. "And yeah, I'm worried about her. She's a good kid."

I thought so, too, once, and I'm paying for my mistake. "She made her choice."

His exhale rushes across the mouthpiece. When has he ever been this annoyed? "Maybe I was wrong."

I scrunch my brow. "About what?"

"You not being stupid."

The line goes dead, and I'm left speechless. What the

hell. How can all this be coming down on me at once? Tino's usually so levelheaded, well, more like cold and calculating, but still. For him to shoot back like that, at me, is out of character. Grabbing my bag from the back, I head to the plane, taking the stairs two by two as the rain picks up.

"Ready for takeoff." My pilot's voice comes over the speaker. "We should just miss the storm rolling in." Within seconds, we're starting down the runway. A perk of owning a private plane is you can take off whenever the mood suits you. I'm better off somewhere far away, getting work done. A moment later we're over "the estate." It's dark now, but I can still picture the taillights as Tino drove her away that night.

Annoyed, I run my hand across my face, as if I can wipe away the memory. Can't she see Conrado's using her? He wanted her for her virginity…fuck. Another thing I screwed up. Does he know? So far, he hadn't taken her that way.

My mind takes me to an ugly place. The one where Iris is having sex but not with me. My thoughts return to that first night in the sleazy motel. How she'd looked away when I came in, trying to pull away from him, her grimace when he touched her. She hadn't acted anything like when she'd been with me, quite the opposite, in fact. I sit up straight. After digging my head out of my ass, free of the cloud of lust, I can see things with more detail. She wasn't with him because she wanted to be, something was forcing the issue.

He holds something of great value. The words echo in my head, I even hear them in Montoya's voice. The truth hits me like a shower of river water. *Shit, she's the "something" of great value.* Slamming a fist into the armrest, I draw my new conclusions from a different deck of cards. *Does she actually have a choice? And, if not, why?* What could Conrado be holding over Iris? Her face shows everything she's feeling, but I've been too pissed, hurt, annoyed, whatever the hell else, to see it.

Realizing she has something so serious she would turn her life over to scum like Conrado, I have to figure out what it is. Will I get any answers if I confront her? There's one person who can dig up the truth, if for no other reason than to prove she can. I pull up Kassy's contact info and connect by FaceTime. The image on the screen freezes, blinks then comes back.

"Can't a girl do yoga without getting interrupted?" Kassy frowns back at me from the monitor, her purple hair folded up in some kind of ponytail on top of her head.

Luckily I've been around her long enough to know how to switch her out of a mood. "I need you to solve a puzzle." I slam the words out without bothering with a hello.

She perks up. "Talk to me." She unfolds from whatever position she was holding and heads to her computer.

"Get me a workup on Iris Gloria."

Raising an eyebrow, she slips into her chair, rolling toward her keyboard while batting a cat off her desk. "Wait, I thought you didn't want me checking into her."

I drag in a long breath. "I didn't want a mark, I wanted the"—*cute, funny, sexy*—"woman herself." That's all she needs to know. "There's something tying her to Conrado Villa, and I need to know what."

"But we hardly found anything on him," she points out. "And you didn't want Tino to follow up."

Shame whips at my chest. I held back information on him. Things that may have gotten us here quicker. Things that might have even led us to bring him into the circle. I'd hated him immediately, and it doubled when Iris came into the picture. "Link him to Gloria's Market, and try again."

The quick glare speaks volumes. Her fingers are slamming down on the keyboard with every stroke. Yeah, she's pissed about me holding out on her. "There's no payroll for him—anywhere." She keeps typing.

"He was working there." My leg is bouncing on par with my anxiety.

"Give me a second." She mumbles a bit in Mandarin. "Only one computer," she announces, after an eternity. "Let me see what I can find."

"Okay. I'll head to town." I leave her to dig while I tell the pilot to change our destination and find a way to land—now. The plane banks as the pilot heads back to the city, instead of the West Coast.

Next, Tino. The phone rings once then three beeps and a *Call Fail* message. I try again. *Beep-beep-beep.* Again. *Beep-beep.* I slam my finger down to end the call. Damn this storm we're flying into. I have to get to Iris.

My hands sting—that's how I figure out I'm digging my nails into my palms. Normally it's twenty-thirty minutes or so, but the sky is pitch-black. According to the weather app, Laredo's under a thunderstorm.

I hit Tino's number again. A single ring. "Come on."

But the line drops again, and I toss the cell on the seat. I'll have to wait until we get there then grab the car and head to Iris.

The phone rings, breaking into my thoughts. I lunge toward the edge of the seat. Kassy. I press the button to answer. "H—"

"Where have you been?" She rushes through, cutting me off.

"Bad weath—"

"I was about to call Tino," she says, barrels through. "You've got to..." The line cuts out. "Piece of shit." The passion in her voice freezes me in place. "I want Tino to track him down and annihilate him," she finishes in a shaky voice. "And I don't give a f—" A second later the screen goes to video. Conrado's hand goes up, and Iris flinches then the line starts to buffer.

"No! You fucking..." Helpless, I sit in the chair, unable to go anywhere, and with no way to make the damn plane go faster. Desperation is clawing at me, and I want to smash my fist into the screen. The scene cuts to Iris hitting the desk, headfirst then cuts off. Rage explodes inside me, burning into every limb and every cell.

The phone chimes. I'm still glaring at the screen when Kassy's message dips down from the top of the screen. *They're going to get her tonight.*

*****

IRIS

Something brought me awake, sitting up to check the dark corners of my room. Nothing. The alarm clock shows one o'clock, so I finally dozed off for an hour or so. I slump back, letting myself plop down on the pillow. Would I manage any sleep tonight?

Heavy pounding on the back door comes through over the rain pelting the roof. Eyes wide open, I bolt out of bed and grab Dad's old baseball bat, squeezing the handle. *It'll be all right. If I go down, I go down swinging.*

Unlocking my bedroom door, I take cautious steps down the hallway to the back. Whoever managed to jump the fence during a storm came up the driveway and through the carport without riling up the neighbor's dog. *Right hand over left.* My pulse echoes against my clammy palms as I tighten my grip on the bat.

"Who's there?" Thunder rolls, and I strain to catch any sound that might give me a clue. Could someone be trying to figure out if the house is empty? What if he, or they, push their way inside. Without a phone line, what can I do? Would the neighbors even hear me over the storm?

"Iris, it's Dante."

Dante's here? Every muscle relaxes. My shoulders sag, not just because he identified himself, but *he* came. Hope and dismay fight to be heard.

"Open the door." Releasing a pent-up breath, I wobble through the last few steps to the doorway.

Flipping the dead bolt, I stop, my fingers hovering over the knob. Tino said he hadn't asked about me. So why is he at the door all of a sudden? Dante didn't just drop me, he all but shoved me in the car when he sent me away. Pain slices across my chest as I picture his furious expression. Thunder cracks overhead, jolting me.

"What do you want?" With my heart thundering, I bite my lip, waiting for an answer I may not like.

"I need to talk to you. Open the door," he insists.

"About?"

"Just open the door, Iris," he demands.

Doubt creeps into me. Should I take the chance? Because believing in him had left me heartbroken. "Iris, I swear, if you don't open this door, I'm going to drag Conrado here to answer my questions."

Gasping, I drop the bat to clatter on the kitchen floor.

"Iris, is he there?" The metal screen protests as he yanks on the knob. "Get your hands off her, you goddamn son of a bitch," he yells over the rain.

Startled, my body jerks. Lord, he thinks I'm here with Conny.

"Stand clear." His voice booms through the door.

"No. Wait, I'm coming." Hands shaking, I struggle with the lock for several seconds. Finally, I pull the door open to find Dante standing in the doorway, gun in hand. My brain amplifies the size of the weapon and I grow even clumsier. Without looking away from my face, he puts the gun into the back of his pants as my boneless fingers continue to fumble with the slide-lock on the screen door.

His gaze runs over me, as if he's trying to make sure everything's okay. As soon as he's in the house, his arms come around me. Crushing me to him, he pushes me back into the kitchen, his lips crashing down on mine.

"Tell me you're okay," he whispers insistently, while his hands run down my arms then come to cup my cheeks.

"Yes, I-I'm fine," I stammer. As fine as I can be after standing there, scared and confused over being pulled out of an exhausted sleep in the middle of the night.

Dante's expression hardens. He stares past me, into the darkness. "Is Conrado here?"

"No."

His gaze shoots back to me. "Where is he?" His anger comes in waves, dashing against me. But I don't have the answer he wants. Olga gave up Dad's apartment two months ago, so I have no clue where he goes any more.

"I don't know." What does he want with Conny anyway? My blood runs cold, and a shiver takes over my body as adrenaline rushes through me.

He cups my arm. "I'm sorry. I was jealous as hell." He sucks in a breath. "And I wasn't thinking straight."

My apprehension and doubt crumble at his words. His arms come around me, holding me tight, as if he'll lose me if he lets go. "Last time, I thought you didn't want to leave Conrado. That you chose him over me."

My eyes could have bulged out at his statement. "No, of course not." The horror in my voice reflects off the back of my throat. "What made—"

"I understand that now." He rubs my back, trying to soothe me. "I realize you think you can't leave." He draws in a deep breath. "But at the time, it hurt, and I didn't deal with it well." The moment hangs between us, with the silence saying more than words ever could. He pulls back then brings his face to mine. "I'm sorry I was such an ass. Please forgive me, baby."

Relief washes through me, leaving me weak at the knees. "Yes." A smile breaks through for the first time in days. "I'm sorry I hurt you. I didn't mean to." He cups my face and kisses me like he hasn't seen me in forever.

"What's he holding over you?"

My eyes go wide. How did he know?

"What did you do?"

This can't be happening. If I had anything sitting in my stomach, I'd be retching at his feet now.

"Nothing," I manage to say, past the gigantic lump in my throat. Unable to face him, I duck, hiding my face, though he wouldn't be able to see my shame in the darkness.

Swinging around, he pulls the gun from the back of his waist and shoves me away. I look up in time to see a figure filling the doorway. Everything happens at once. I don't even have time to scream before I hit the cabinet. I suck in a breath, but the air is so dense with moisture I nearly choke. Lightning flashes across Dante as he points his weapon at the intruder. His features could be chiseled from stone with all the angles in shadow.

"What the hell?" The screen door opens as he lowers his gun.

"I hung around." Tino's voice reaches me from around the door.

"You were right, man," Dante admits in an apologetic tone. "I was stupid."

"I know." Stepping into the kitchen, he looks my way, though he can't possibly see me in the dark. "You took care of mine when I couldn't," he says. Dante gives him a brief nod before they both turn to me.

Dante reaches out a hand to me. Weak, I pull away from the solid wood supporting me and drag myself over. "Sorry, baby, but we need to go. Now." The rain's coming even harder, covering the sound of a car going by until the driver hits the gas farther up the block. "We *need* to get you out of here." He twines his fingers through mine.

"What do you mean?" I frown.

"Conrado's coming for you, and I have no idea who he's got with him."

Icy threads stretch down my back, forcing out a gasp. They plan to finish what they started this afternoon.

"That might be them," Dante warns, tightening his hold on my hand. Meanwhile, Tino straightens, turning on his heel as he pushes the door open. "No. Wait." Dante curls a hand into a fist. "It may not be them." He shakes his head and faces Tino. "I'd rather you be here to keep Iris safe."

"Okay, then." Tino pulls a weapon from inside his coat and another from his back. Fear claws at me as the walls close in.

Reality crashes down around me. What will Conny do if he finds me gone? What if he trashes the house?

"I need to get my phone." I try pulling away, but Dante tightens his arms around me and keeps moving.

"We can replace it," he assures me.

"No, please." I shift, trying to wiggle out of his grasp. Releasing an exasperated breath, he loosens his hold.

Tino flips the light switch and frowns. "Power's out. Must be the storm."

My face flames, even in the darkness. "No, I haven't had electricity in a while." They both stare at me. Taking the opportunity, I slip out of Dante's arms and rush down the hall to my room. I snatch up the phone, holding it to my chest then hurry back to find them exchanging words quietly.

"I'll pull the car into the drive." Dante puts an arm around me, crushing me to him for a kiss before he strides away.

Tino and I stay by the door. "You okay?" he asks, without taking his gaze off the surroundings.

"Yes." Somehow I manage to get the single word past the lump in my throat. Seconds tick by. "You were outside?"

"Down the street."

"Why?" My heart is thundering away in my chest.

"You're important to him." He scans the entire backyard, stopping an extra second at the extension on the carport.

"I don't know about that." I can't assume anything.

Tino does that inch-by-inch turn to face me. "The guy went out in a storm, putting himself in danger of being ambushed, to keep you safe. If you knew what kind of a selfish son of a bitch he's become over the years, you'd understand just how important you are."

Tears prick the back of my eyes. No words can explain how humbling this moment is for someone in my situation.

I'm glad I can spend tonight with him. Conny isn't going to let me go without a fight, and I have no idea how Dante will react to my story. The best I can do is figure out a plan to run, and with any luck, Dante will help me get away. At least I'll have a handful of memories to help me get through wherever life leads me after that.

*****

CONRADO

"He's there, dude," Iz blurts out with urgency. "He's there." Like I don't fuckin' see his ride up ahead. "What's Dante doing at Iris's house?"

"The bitch double-crossed me." It pisses me off even more that I have to spell it out for him between clenched teeth.

"You think so?" Iz's eyes shoot open, like he can't believe what I said.

"How else is he gonna be there?" I spit back.

"You think she gave it up?" he asks quietly, dragging his palms down his pants leg.

"How the fuck would I know if they're fucking?" If Dante's at her house now, he isn't gonna stop at a blow. And if she did give it up, I can kiss that dime goodbye. "Fuck!" I slam my fist against the steering wheel over and over. The bitch really did set me up. She's been out to get me since the beginning. I grab the wheel, just to have something to squeeze. Iris didn't just set me up, she stole my score. She figures I can't touch her if she's with Dante.

"If they've been hooking up...what if she told him about this afternoon?" Iz bites at his thumbnail.

Iz has a point. And it all fits with what I'm thinking. If she's got Dante, he's gonna be batshit pissed about this afternoon. He's got no right because that pussy was mine to begin with, but he ain't gonna see it that way.

"You think she told him what we did?"

"If she did, we're blown." I hit the gas, just in case. The worst part about this is losing my chance with Dante. I take the turn with screeching tires as I drift the POS I'm driving. Whatever. A couple of blocks and I'll be outta here. That's all that matters.

"So what happens now?" Iz's voice is shaky. He probably knows we're in a bad spot but can't figure it out how it ends. He's also annoying the fuck outta me.

"Shut up, man. Let me think." I know the guy has muscle that takes care of shit for him. I can still see that dude staring down at me and Iz, and my throat knots up. If he comes after us, we are fucked. I could give them Iz, but I need him. And really, if they go after him, he'll flip on me. Damn, I'm gonna lose the deal and more over that piece of—

"Rad." Iz's voice is high and scared.

I look up in time to swerve, passing some shithead that stopped at the corner. Any other time I woulda stopped and kicked the shit outta that guy. I can't take the chance that Dante or his muscle shows up. I gotta focus on getting me and Iz outta this mess.

"Toss the phones."

"What?" Iz's voice goes higher.

"They can track us through the phones."

"Oh."

I need to get the money, without it I can't get far. I spin another corner when it hits me, and red-hot rage tears through my gut. I can't go back for the safe. He'll figure that's what I'd do and catch me there. Fuck.

I whip into a parking lot and roll down to a dark corner. Whatever I'm gonna do, I gotta move fast and I need that money. Iz has enough sense not to say a word; I can feel him watching me as I stare out the window.

Leaning back, I realize I got one option left. Dante won't hurt my mom if he catches her, he might even buy her excuse for why she's taking the money. So now it's up to her. She owes me after the crap I had to clean up for her.

Dropping the car into gear, I head out to find her.

CHAPTER EIGHTEEN

IRIS

We drove across town, through a high-end neighborhood, to a house that probably cost more money than I would earn in my lifetime. The half bath, where I stopped to wash up, is the size of my bedroom, with towels so plush my fingers nearly disappear in the fibers. This is how Dante lives, and his home is nowhere near the store.

Reality's creeping in again, so I wrap my arms around myself. I left my parents' home in an old nightshirt and bare feet, my only possession a phone with no service. If it didn't hold the only family pictures still in existence, I would have left it behind also. Pain slices through me. When will I go back there? Will it ever be my family's home again? Taking a deep, calming breath, I turn the knob and step out.

"Iris," Dante calls from somewhere down the hall. Curling my hands, I follow his voice down the wide hallway to an office. He's behind an enormous wooden desk with intricate carvings. To his left, he has a monitor bigger than the TV in my room. *Lord, I can't be comparing everything if I want to stop feeling like a doormat.*

His features are relaxed as he holds out a hand, calling me next to him. The sight makes me smile. I circle the desk to find he's online with a woman.

"This is Kassy." Pushing a corner, he adjusts the monitor at an angle.

"Hey, girl." Kassy's probably in her late twenties, with blonde hair and highlights ending halfway down her chest in a deep purple matching her cat-eye glasses.

"Hello," I reply, trying my best to smile while wondering who exactly she is.

"I'm glad you're safe." Her almond eyes show sympathy.

My gaze immediately goes to Dante. Considering her choice of words, my insides start squirming, and I duck my head.

He pulls me over, bringing me to sit in his lap. "Kassy is my IT specialist. She keeps all my personal things secure."

"I'm sorry, Iris." Glancing up, I brace myself for pity I half expect. "I thought Dante told you about me." She glares at him before switching back to me, her expression losing the harsh lines.

"I'm here, too." Tino's voice comes from the speaker.

Kassy turns to her keyboard then Tino's profile fills half the monitor, the car seat's headrest peeking out in the background.

Dante gives my hand a light squeeze, calling my attention back to him. "I need you to tell us about Conrado."

For the second time tonight, I'm glad I'm on an empty stomach. I've been dreading the moment when I'll have to tell him everything. And now, suddenly, three people will hear my confession. I press my eyes closed. Will this night never end?

"I saw the video, Iris." Dante's voice is steady, not giving away what he may be feeling. What did he think when he saw me looking over my shoulder nervously, while taking stacks of money out of the safe? Did he wonder how he could be with a petty thief? Tears trickle down my face as shame takes over.

"Please don't be embarrassed," Kassy cuts in. "Girl, you're stronger than you imagine," she says adamantly. "Trust me when I tell you, most people would crumble having to go through what you suffered."

Tino turns, his full attention on me.

"Talk to me," Dante coaxes. "Let me help you out of whatever trouble you're in."

I want so hard to believe that can happen. This nightmare can end, and I can get my life back. Gulping in air, I gather my thoughts and explain what happened. "Conny and his mother set me up." Is this the best way to start my explanation? How do I defend myself? How do I make them believe I never stole anything in my life?

"My father disappeared last year. He left the store and never came home. I didn't even realize it because we'd had a bad fight…" Shame piles on, making me jittery. "The things I said to him…"

Dante's arms come around me. "I'm sure he understands," Dante murmurs, pulling some napkins from a drawer.

I clutch one as if my life depends on it. "He-he said I probably wished he'd been the one to die and not my mother." I bring the napkin to my face. "I did." I hang my head, my voice barely a whisper. "And I told him so, to his face." I've held that guilt for so long, it burned into my soul. Sharing the secret restarts the fire.

"Maybe we can wait until tomorrow." Kassy's understanding tone both humbles me and gives me the will to keep going.

"I'm okay," I sniff. "I didn't find out he was missing until days later since I'd been avoiding him. Olga, his girlfriend, came looking for me. She was a mess." I wiped my nose. "Even hit the back of the carport when she came in. But she managed to do a police report on his disappearance. There's just not a lot they can do in these cases."

Dante clears his expression, obviously familiar with having people disappear in Nuevo Laredo.

"She said she thought he was being held for ransom. She'd had some big fight with Conny, so she sent me to get the money out of the safe and bring it to the house."

"No one called," he says, realizing the setup.

I purse my lips, shaking my head. "I feel like such an idiot for believing her." I let my hands fall to my lap in defeat. "The money's gone. My father's gone. And now she disappears for days at a time, dropping in unexpectedly whenever she feels like it." I swallow hard, knowing I have to tell him everything. "Conny…" I couldn't continue with the rest.

"He's a fucking pig," Kassy spits out.

Bitter tears threaten as memories pummel me from

where I stuffed them at the back of my mind. Being thrown, my clothes ripping, desperately screaming for a dad who would never come, and through it all, Conny's laughter.

"After…the first time, I told Conny I was going to call the police."

Dante's hold grows firm.

"But Olga had already filed a police report on the "theft." He showed me the recordings: the fight then my father disappears, and a couple of days later, I'm taking his money out of the safe in the middle of the night." I twist the napkin around my fingers until Dante places his hands over mine. "He pointed out anyone who saw the tape would think I was stealing. And that's just what they'd tell the police." I sniff hard. "I was scared. The truth is, I kept hearing noises, and I thought someone else was in the building." I wipe my nose. "There I am, clear as day, pulling money out of the safe." The tears start again. "More cash than I ever imagined my father would keep on hand." Dante pulls out another napkin. "I look guilty as hell," I explain between sniffles. "I kept checking over my shoulder because I was afraid someone would catch me."

"We can check into that tomorrow. If things look bad, we'll hire the best lawyer in the country to defend you," Dante assures me.

With that burden lifted, I could drift off on a cloud. For someone to believe me without hesitation is a marvel. Hopefully they'll have some luck setting things right.

Dante shifts me in his hold. "How can Conrado come up with a hundred and fifty thousand dollars?"

I push up in his lap. "He's been siphoning money from the store. I don't think it would be that much." Wringing my fingers, I run some rough numbers. "He's fired nearly everyone, so he's saving on salaries, and he hasn't paid our vendors."

"Would that be enough?" Kassy sits back in her chair, scrunching her brow.

"Well…" I raise my shoulders. "If you include what Dad had in there from before, maybe."

Dante frowns. "Where's he keeping the money?"

"No clue." I'm no help at all.

"The cash is in the safe," Kassy supplies. We both turn to stare at the screen.

"What?" My jaw nearly drops. He's had the money at the store the entire time, and yet he hasn't paid the bills.

Dante squeezes my hand. "Are you sure?"

"Saw him pull stacks of money from the safe on a video clip from this afternoon."

Dante turns to me. "Have you checked in there?"

I shake my head. "I don't really go in the office." I hike a shoulder. It wouldn't make a difference if I did. "Besides, Conny changed the combination."

"Did you see him open the safe?" Tino asks.

"No." She turns to the keyboard, clicking away for a bit. "The guy was smart enough to clear the security footage, but he kept some files on you." My face burns just thinking about what's on those clips.

The scene comes up, and Conny's whooping as he shows off the stacks of money. He brought two bundles out and kissed each one before putting them on the desk.

"Dude, you sure we got enough?" Iz leans forward and frowns.

"Don't worry, man." Conny waves a hand. "We're close, then we hit easy street." He gets a wild look in his eyes. "These people are talking millions. Millions."

"Fuck, dude." Iz throws his hands up in the air. "If you'd closed the deal for this chick…"

"I know, man." Conrado stomps a boot down. "I was this close. *This* close." He holds up his thumb and index finger. Shaking his head, he tightens his lips, muttering something to himself.

"You know what?" He turns to Iz, who's still drooling over the money. "Get Iris the fuck in here."

Every muscle in Dante's body goes rigid as Iz disappears off the screen and Conny puts the money back in the safe. He may not have seen the rest of the video, but he knows what's going to happen.

Biting my lip, I turn to him. "Are you sure you want to see this?"

He looks over to where the bruise is forming next to my eye. "Yes."

*****

DANTE

Seconds tick by as I wrestle with a wave of anger. I only saw a snippet of the video earlier, before I lost signal, but it was enough. There's a hollow in my chest because I know what that asshole is going to do to her. And all I can do is sit here, in my own personal hell, and watch what happens.

Iris's voice comes in from beyond the screen. She's cautious, clearly wanting to keep her distance, so this isn't the first time she's dealt with him. What I wouldn't give if I could reach in and pull her back.

The other guy, Conrado's boy, is there, too. His hands are on her, and I want to tear his throat out for touching her.

My conscience is drawn in. Every time Conrado says my name, a rail spike goes through my gut. I did this. Why didn't I cut him loose when I had the chance? Because I don't let anything stop me from getting what I want—and I wanted Iris Gloria for myself.

The side of her beautiful face hits the desk, and I flinch. I've seen much worse, done much worse, and it's never bothered me. But this is Iris, and that makes all the difference.

"I won't help you screw Dante over." The hammer comes down again. Even though she's in obvious danger, she's trying to protect me, while I immediately condemned her as a traitor and sent her away. I'm a fucking bastard, and I don't deserve her.

Iris sets her hand on my chest. "I'm okay," she whispers. I squeeze her tighter.

The clip ends, and I drag in a painful breath. "That piece of shit is never going to touch you again." My voice is rough as I make the solemn promise. "I'll make sure of it."

She swallows hard, her eyes filling with a trust I plan to earn some day.

"Has the alarm at the store been deactivated?" Tino's gruff voice breaks in, reminding me we're not alone.

Kassy flips to another screen. "No."

"I'll cover the money." Tino starts the car. "And I'll send someone over to the house, in case anyone shows."

"Yeah," I agree. "Though I think it was them when we heard that car take off."

"Which means we're blown." Kassy scrunches her face.

"Then I can go home?"

Kassy sits up so fast she sends a cat running. "Don't you dare."

I tighten my hold. "You want to leave?"

Iris meets my gaze. "I need clothes for work." Leaning forward, she stares at her toes, wiggling them. "I didn't even grab shoes when I left, and I have to go in tomorrow."

My frown is immediate.

"You can't," Kassy cuts in.

"But I need to open," she insists. "It's still my family's store."

I hadn't thought much past getting her out of there. "Can anyone else open the store?" I understand her desire to keep her father's legacy alive, but she needs to lie low until we can get this mess under control.

"Well, yes." Her voice holds a world of uncertainty. "Carol helps me, but she and Oscar are the only employees right now."

"Call and tell her you're sick." I run my palm along her side, trying to comfort her. "There's a lot of work to do, and I need you safe."

Biting her bottom lip, she makes her decision. "Okay." Her resigned tone cuts deep. "But I'll need to borrow a phone." She holds her cell up, rocking her wrist from side to side. "No service." She puts her thumb to the home button. "But it's full of my parents' pictures." She flips through, a small smile on her face.

Despite everything I've managed to amass, I feel so small right now. Insignificant. She has no car, no electricity, no phone, and with her life falling apart, she can still find happiness in the memories at hand.

"Kassy can take care of your phone," I whisper. "Just give her your number." The monitor reflects in the tears gathering at her lashes. She leans back and looks away. Pride or shame? I've become so jaded I can't tell. I'm used to people jumping at the chance for a freebie. And the one person I want to help is having an issue with taking what's offered.

"You can keep a list of expenses if it'll make you feel better," I offer.

Kassy watches from the screen, but I ignore her reaction.

"Meanwhile, you can work on getting your employees back," I continue. "I'll front you the money to pay them and the vendors you owe. We'll settle up once things are back to normal."

"My tab might run a little high." She looks up, pressing her lips together in a slight grimace.

It's all I can do to contain myself. "It'll be alright."

Iris leans into me and rattles off the number.

"Here we go." Kassy grins. "You have phone service now. And I found you a personal shopper," she announces. "I'm sending you her contact number. Call or text her with your sizes. She can deliver a whole new wardrobe by midmorning."

Hmm. Okay, maybe clothes could have waited. The thought of having her in nothing but a thin cotton T-shirt...

"Thank you." She exhales, her body going limp, like she's just put down the weight of the world.

"Why don't you try to get some rest," I suggest.

"Okay," she whispers against my shoulder.

"I have a few things to discuss with the guys." She

shuffles out, closing the door behind her. After a handful of seconds, I turn back to the monitors.

"Caitlin's on board," Tino barks.

"Send a plane if you need to."

"Already did," he says with authority. "She'll be here in the morning to crack the safe."

"You got to her just in time." Kassy blows out a breath. "It was them you heard. I tracked down two cell phones where he sent copies of the clip. They're a couple of yards from each other, about a mile from the house."

Tino grunts. "They ditched 'em."

"Probably." She exhales in a rush. "But with no damn cameras, I can't be positive."

"Conrado claimed to have a crew that would support his venture. His friend, Israel, has family with some background, but I can't find anything to make me believe they'd work for him."

"Something about this whole thing stinks," Tino agrees. "I'll ask around, see what I can find."

"I'll see what I can dig up on my side."

"Okay. Get eyes on the store. I want new locks, new codes, new passwords, and a new combination on the safe. I need the guys fully armed and ready for anything before Iris steps foot in there again."

"You got it." Tino disconnects.

"Gotcha." Kassy's face fills the screen.

"Find anything you can on these police reports," I add before she logs off. "I need to know where we stand."

CHAPTER NINETEEN

DANTE

I walk out of the office and open the bedroom door. Within two steps I know she's not in here. Flipping on the light, I confirm the room is empty. Frowning, I double back, craning my neck to glance into the living room. Sure enough, she's curled up on the couch, her legs covered with the throw pillows I'd always found so useless.

It hadn't occurred to me to talk to her about where to sleep. When we got in, I left her to wash up and went directly to the office without showing her around. *Talk about being a bad host.* I drag in a breath, letting the unexpected pressure in my chest disappear.

Taking careful steps, I go around the coffee table and lean down to work my arms under her. She barely gives me time to straighten up before she tenses.

"I'm awake," she says, looking toward the ground.

Yes, I could have easily put her down, but damn if I'm not enjoying having her in my arms.

"Shhh. I've got you." I maneuver around the end of the coffee table while she puts her hand on my shoulder. "Sorry, I didn't get to show you around earlier."

"It's okay," she says with understanding. "I didn't want to assume anything."

"Ah. I guess I'll have to assume for both of us."

"Silly."

"Sweetheart, a better man would ask if you wanted to take a guest room." I turn back toward my room, taking each step with utter confidence. "Unfortunately for you, I am not *a better man*." She chuckles. "I'm the kinda man that's wondering if you're flashing something like those pretty purple panties you had on the other day."

"Dan-te," she says with mock disapproval. The amusement in her voice gives her away.

I walk into the bedroom, my strides getting longer as I get closer to the bed. Lowering her on my side of the king-size bed, I drop a quick kiss on her lips. "Get under the covers and scoot over." She moves to the other pillow, watching me undress in record time before turning off the light and joining her.

Within minutes, Iris is asleep against my chest, her legs entwined with mine. I can't stop touching her, yet I'm afraid I'll wake her up. She deserves this moment of peace because she's going to need all her strength when I tell her I know where to find her father.

*****

Thank you for reading STEALING IRIS.

You can read Tino and Bonnie's story in Saving Bonnie.

What happens when an innocent café owner finds herself in danger and a stone-cold killer comes to her rescue? They strike a deal, of course. Keep reading for the first scene.

If you want heroes on the side of the law, try Desire & Deception, Book 1 in the **DANGEROUS DESIRES** series.

Now, on to Tino's story…

EXCERPT FROM SAVING BONNIE

Tino

Lightning streaks across the night sky, illuminating a shadow with a panicked face across the street. He looks left, right then leans over to whisper to his partner before checking again. Fool doesn't realize the danger isn't on the street. I'm on the second floor.

"What've you got?" Marshal Cord Benson's voice comes across the radio.

"Burglary in progress," his partner, Frank, replies from a car down the street. "Two males, mid-twenties."

Burglars. Scrambling around like ants–amateurs. One looks like he's got some experience, but the other, with the round face, still has his cherry.

"Hold position." Law enforcement, always dealing with nonessentials.

"What the hell, Tino," Frank barks over the radio. "These guys are about to break into the café."

"Aww, shit," Cord cuts in. "What's the status, Frank?"

"Suspects checked the door and windows. Now they're in front of the gate, trying to look inconspicuous. Gonna wait for one to go over the fence so I can move in," Frank reports.

"I'm headin' in." Cord's voice comes across, uneven. He's already on the move.

"Hold. Your. Position," I shoot back.

"Criminal or fugitive apprehension is one of the most dangerous parts of law enforcement." Spoken like a true marshal. "One man can't—"

In the years I hunted men, tracking those who carried out atrocities, I always hunted alone. Cord thinks I'll get involved in apprehension—this is exactly why he's sitting south side. He's better off watching the apartment where Conrado Villa's buddy lives while we look out for his mother.

I'm not used to working with law, at least not honest law. With their nonstop chatter, to "keep things lively," I'm ready to cut them both loose.

"Hold on, man," Frank interrupts while the skinny guy goes over the three-foot fence, nearly losing his pants as he lands. The heavier one uses the chain link as footholds and gets his shoe stuck. Just then, skinny realizes the gate isn't locked.

Damn, stupid criminals. If they weren't so common, high-end services, like the one I work for, wouldn't exist.

Frank scoffs into the radio. "I think we're good."

"*Suuure.*" Cord's got that note in his voice that makes me want to punch him. "What's a little B&E among friends, right?"

Turns out this stakeout is a test of my patience. If it weren't for Dante, I'd do the world a favor and get rid of this asshole. Three days of his shit. I should put in for sainthood! If God existed, I'd believe he was fucking with me, I muse while lying in the balcony of the Catholic church across the street from the café. Thanks to a "generous donation," the area has been blocked off, so I can stay out of sight while waiting. Intel has Olga Villa coming by at least once or twice a week, but so far, she's a no-show.

"Building's empty," I point out. Bonnie Bustos, or Bunny, as Iris and Dante call her, is out. She's not due back for at least a couple of hours. "They're gonna head back to Frank. He can stop 'em then." Though Frank's got a badge, he understands what goes on at the border, and why we do the things we do. "Just don't fuck with my stakeout."

"Yes, sir, sir," Cord shoots back with condescension.

Great. Now I'll have to put up with Cord being an asshole for hours.

"You call if you need a hand, bud." The last part is obviously not for me.

"Nah, they're punks," Frank adds, dismissing the offer. "Shouldn't need more than a taser."

"Great. Don't want Ms. Bonnie Boo-hooin' if they take anything."

The first inklings of exasperation crop up. In my defense, I've spent three days listening to his bullshit about Bonnie. He's been playing up her name way past the joke dying. It started with Busty then Busty's got back. Frank had to tell him her name's pronounced boo-stows. So he started on Bonnie Boo, needing a boo, and now he graduated to Busty's got boo-ty. Not that the guy's wrong—on any account. Just the sight of the woman will remind any man he's alive.

Though if he figures out she goes by Bunny and starts on that, I'm going to kill him.

A light stretches out along the ground like another pothole in the narrow parking lot's buckling asphalt. Dumb and dumber must have gotten through the door.

My phone vibrates in my back pocket. I have half a mind to ignore it, but Frank may want to go offline. Reaching for it, I pull the screen around to see who's on the line. Kassy, the IT and security specialist. Frowning, I hit the home button.

"You all right?" she asks, getting straight to the point.

"Yeah." I check the area again, in case I missed something. "Why?"

"Montoya got one of his vibes, and—"

"Oh-oh," Frank exaggerates the syllables. What the hell is going on now? "We got a problem," he confirms.

Gathering patience, I force a question out between clenched teeth. "What?"

"She's back." Grabbing the binoculars, I focus on the car coming in at the end of the street. Sure enough, the electric-blue Mini Cooper has a damn Uber sticker on the windshield.

It's times like this where Montoya disturbs my goddamn calm. How the hell can Dante's business partner be ahead of us when he's on the ranch a couple hundred miles away?

"I have movement," Frank announces. "They left someone in the car. And they're on the phone, likely giving a heads-up."

The Uber stops in front of the café, and the driver fully turns in his seat. The door opens and a pair of white, high-heeled sandals pops out above the door, followed by Miss Bonnie herself. White ruffled top, little peach shorts that hug her ass, and some lime-green, foam sandals they use for pedicures.

Goddammit.

The fucking driver takes his time pulling away, checking his mirrors for one last look at Miss Bustos's assets. Fuck if I don't want to just go push the car down the street on my own.

"What's wrong?" Kassy whispers.

"Two guys in the building, and she's back early."

"Oh damn. Why is she early?" Her nails do a rapid-fire tap across the keyboard then come to a sudden stop. "*Baka*! Forgot, there's no security system. I'm blind," she finishes, sounding helpless. Kassy did the research on Bonnie. Every Sunday she takes an Uber to her mom's house, coming home after ten o'clock. For whatever reason, she chooses today to break routine.

"So what are we doing?" Frank drops a tangled mess on my shoulders.

I don't break protocol—ever. It's kept me alive, and from being discovered, for all these years.

A shadow of unease settles over me, driving me to check on Miss Bonnie. She's Iris's best friend, practically a sister. And Iris, one of the few people I give a damn about, lost her mother and still has to deal with her missing father. Not sure how she'll take losing someone else, especially when I could prevent it.

"No…not on my watch!" Instinct kicks in as I spring up, turn on my heel, and fly down the stairs and jump across to the next landing.

"Got your back." Frank's voice comes in low and meaningful. I know I can count on him to watch what he says around Cord.

I'm breaking cover, if this goes wrong, neither of them can be involved. I jam the earbud in as I bust out the door and streak across the street. "May need you."

"Got ya," Kassy gives a curt acknowledgment as a disgruntled cat complains in the background.

With one hand, I grip the top bar and kick off of the body of the fence. Redirecting my momentum, I'm up in the air, hurdling the fence. Gravel. Unexpected but I stick the landing and I'm clear. Drizzle starts to fall—perfect, what else can go wrong? Hopefully, with the rain, anyone in the area will decide to stay in tonight. If not, Frank's gonna have to step up for as long as he can.

"Maybe they'll hear her and run off," Kassy suggests hopefully.

I dash along the side of the building, through the parking area, but somehow I know that isn't gonna happen. The closer I get, the more my gut is screaming at me that things are gonna go sideways.

I sidle along the edge of the kitchen, blending into the darkness, and peer into the corner of the window. The jerk-offs are across the building, in the dining area, facing me. Bonnie's in the kitchen, frozen in place as skinny raises a Beretta nine mil, by the looks of it. "Never killed anyone before." He grins and looks Bunny over as if he's got a prize coming.

"Call maintenance," I mutter to Kassy. "I'm going to work."

Want more? Read <u>Saving Bonnie</u>

Books by Sahara Roberts

Dangerous Desire Series

Desire & Deception

Tessa agreed to make her last night in Mexico memorable, but she didn't expect to wake up on the floor of a cartel safe-house. **Kris** must claim the fiery redhead to keep her alive while he works to take down the cartel from the inside.

Secrets & Seduction

Monica acts as an informant in the cartel-run town. She expects the danger. She doesn't expect the heated rush of desire for **Andres**, a cartel horse trainer...especially when that desire grows into something deeper and far more complicated.

Temptation & Treachery

Celeste presents a buttoned-up, secretive, exterior but cold and calculating, **Rio**, melts every barrier. Imagine his surprise when he discovers she's a cartel leader's daughter...and she's pregnant with Rio's baby.

About the Author

Sahara Roberts spends her days dealing with international trade issues (the legal kind) and her evenings writing romance. She is currently working on the 2nd book of the Blood Ties series.

Sahara lives in South Texas with her husband, who she lovingly refers to as Brat, and three furry overlords. She enjoys cooking, baking, and cake decorating, but she would certainly prefer to have someone else do the dishes.

Sign up for Sahara's newsletter:

https://sahararoberts.com/newsletter

Like Sahara Roberts on Facebook:

https://www.facebook.com/SaharaRobertsAuthor

Follow Sahara on Instagram:

https://www.instagram.com/sahararoberts/

Visit Sahara's website for her current booklist:

https://sahararoberts.com/

Made in the USA
Monee, IL
12 September 2020

40829482R00118